"Sophie, this is my daughter Lucy," Lark said. "Lucy, say hi to Sophie."

"Hi," the little girl said politely.

Oh, boy. Her head started to pound, little red spots playing in blotches before her eyes.

Sophie's heart somehow rose to touch her tongue, then thudded all the way to her toes.

A pretty, blonde and blue-eyed girl stood before her, lips pulled back in the widest smile Sophie had ever seen, eyes dancing.

Waiting for her to say hello back. Anything other than the jaw-hanging-open expression she guessed she was sporting right now.

No. Surely he would have said if he had a daughter.

Sophie's mouth went dry. She wanted to run. To turn and close her eyes and forget she'd ever been attracted to Lark.

Because she couldn't deal with this. Not now. *Because this was what she'd run away from.* Having to deal with situations like this.

Because she couldn't face up to little people. *Especially* little ones who were the same age as the child she'd lost. The child she'd voluntarily dismissed all those years ago.

Dear Reader

Returning to the place where you grew up can be an important turning point for many people, and that's certainly true for my heroine, Sophie Baxter. But as she comes home her hero, Lark Anderson, moves across the world, far away from his own home, in a bid to start afresh.

In New Zealand, the place where I am so fortunate to live, Sophie and Lark fall in love surrounded by horses and open fields. While they both battle with what has happened to them in the past, their bond makes them confront their issues and forge a new life together.

Horses are a great passion of mine, and I hope you enjoy reading about my gorgeous cowboy and the horses he owns. To me, there is nothing sexier than a man who knows his way around a horse—a man who can communicate with such a large, powerful animal in a kind, understanding way. If that sounds like your kind of hero, then I just know you will love reading this story as much as I enjoyed writing it.

Soraya Lane

RODEO DADDY

BY
SORAYA LANE

First published in Great Britain 2011
by Mills & Boon, an imprint of Harlequin (UK) Limited,
Eton House, 18-24 Paradise Road, Richmond, Surrey TW9 1SR

© Soraya Lane 2011

ISBN: 978 0 263 22122 0

Writing romance for The Cherish™ Series is truly a dream come true for **Soraya Lane**. An avid book reader and writer since her childhood, Soraya describes becoming a published author as 'the best job in the world', and hopes to be writing heart-warming, emotional romances for many years to come.

Soraya lives with her own real-life hero on a small farm in New Zealand, surrounded by animals and with an office overlooking a field where their horses graze.

For my wonderful father, Craig.
After years of my begging for a pony as a child,
it got to the point where he couldn't say no any longer,
and I will always be grateful for his generosity in
indulging my love for horses. It is only fitting, then,
that my first cowboy book is for my dad.

CHAPTER ONE

SOPHIE BAXTER tapped her fingers against the steering wheel as she drove carefully down the gravel road. It was almost dark and the road was slippery, the ground turned dangerous and sludgy beneath the tires.

She had forgotten what it was like to drive in the country, especially in bad weather. She'd spent too long cruising along perfect city streets.

Sophie's eyes strained as she peered hard through the windscreen. The snow had given way to a sleet-rain mixture that was making it hard to see.

What on earth—?

She slammed on her brakes as a man's silhouette appeared in front of her, arms waving above his head, urging her to stop.

Her car slid as she swerved to avoid him.

Sophie shut her eyes. No, please no! She gripped the steering wheel, forced her eyes to open again and watched as her car traveled sideways in slow motion, before finally grinding to a halt.

Her heart was pounding hard, beating in her ears, in her throat, everywhere. Then, as her eyes started to focus again, she saw a flash of something dark darting in front of the car.

Could it have been…?

A horse. A horse was loose on the road.

She fumbled for her handbag and pulled out her phone, hand shaking as she dialed the emergency number.

"What is the nature of your emergency? Fire, ambulance or police?"

Sophie caught her breath long enough to listen to the calm tone on the other end of the line. "Police," she said.

There was a moment's silence, before the line clicked again.

"Police, how can we assist?"

Sophie let her head loll back on the headrest, trying to calm her still-racing heart. Jeez, she'd almost hit a man, then just about taken out a horse!

"I need to report a horse loose on the road," she told the person on the other end, voice shaking. "There's poor visibility. I almost collided with it and the man attempting to catch it."

She finished giving the operator her location and almost leaped out of her skin at a tap on the window.

Damn it! Her heart was racing all over again. She recognized the figure she'd almost run over.

And he looked mad.

Wet and mad.

She wound down her window, about to apologize, but he didn't give her the chance.

"You going to sit there all day, or are you going to help?"

Sophie recoiled at the sharpness of his words. Even his deep American drawl wasn't enough to distract her. How dare he!

"I could have killed you," she told him, angry now. "What were you doing standing in the middle of the road?"

He scowled at her, hands planted on his hips. "I was trying to stop you from plowing into a horse, *actually.*"

If Sophie hadn't been so annoyed with his tone she would have laughed. Seriously, who exactly did he think he was?

The guy was tall, well over six foot, and he was handsome, even if she was loathe to admit it. She could tell that, in spite of the dark, even though she could only just make out his features. His dark hair was plastered to his head, he was soaked through, and he was mad. Hands on hips, brooding kind of mad.

But still, rude was rude. Being handsome was not an excuse.

Sophie watched as he sighed, clearly realizing that she was far from impressed at being told off. He pushed a hand through his hair to stop it from trailing onto his forehead. His shoulders fell.

"I'm sorry, that was rude."

Yep, sure was, but she appreciated the apology.

"What I meant to say was that I'd appreciate your help, if you don't mind getting wet." He gestured at his own body. "Before you came along I almost had her. Now she's loose again."

Sophie sighed. Maybe he wasn't so bad after all. She'd probably given him a hell of a shock almost bowling him over, and a horse on the loose would be stressful for anyone.

"It's okay. I'll help." She rummaged in the back for her waterproof jacket and hauled it on before getting out of the car. "I'm with the local animal shelter, so it's no problem."

The guy looked relieved, a tight smile visible on his face. "Thank you." It made him look less guilty and more of a good guy.

She pulled up the hood on her jacket, braced against the cold. "I've already phoned it in to the police. We'll have help soon."

He groaned. Face-falling-into-his-hands kind of groan.

"This is not my night," he muttered.

She raised an eyebrow in question, before realizing he couldn't see. Why wouldn't he want the police involved? "Is there a problem?"

He shook his head, striding ahead toward the horse. "Let's just try to catch these horses and load them onto my truck, okay?"

At least he was being marginally politer now.

Sophie followed. "How many are we talking about?"

The guy pointed. "Three in that field by the fence there, and the one that's loose."

She looked at the horses. "Why don't we catch the group first, bring them over and start loading them. She might follow."

He stopped. Looked back at her, then started to nod. "Why didn't I think of that?"

Lark Anderson looked over the woman who'd almost run him over and who was now his unlikely savior. He shouldn't have been so rude to her, but she'd sure scared the life from him.

He glanced at her as they walked side by side toward the group of nervous horses, but her features were almost impossible to make out. She was tall, for a woman, and slender. Her outline in the near dark showed a slim woman with long hair in a ponytail, but beyond that it was too hard to see.

"So do you make a habit of working with your horses in the dark?"

She said it with a laugh but it made Lark's skin prickle.

Even so, he wasn't going to bite.

"Not usually, no," he said through gritted teeth. "But then it's not every day a fence is left mangled for a horse to get caught in, either."

She almost came to a stop, looked across at him, then resumed her pace. "Sorry."

He shrugged and tucked his chin against his chest as another icy gust of wind slapped against his cheeks.

"You're not from around here, are you?"

"What gave it away?" he asked. "My weird accent?"

This time she did stop. "Are you always this rude?"

Lark shut his eyes for a heartbeat and sighed, pleased she couldn't see his face properly. "I'm sorry. It's been a long night."

She didn't say anything.

"Let's just say that adjusting to woolen socks and numb toes is harder than you'd think."

She laughed. He was pleased that she was laughing at him

rather than walking away, and he couldn't have blamed her for getting back in her car, blasting on the heat and driving away.

"As opposed to?"

This time Lark laughed. "Would you believe it if I told you a cowboy hat in California?"

He stopped a few feet from one of the horses and held his hand up slightly to tell her to do the same. Lark slowly reached for the horse, slipping a rope around her neck before she could dance sideways away from him. "Whoa, girl, you're okay. It's all right."

"So I take it you're the rodeo rider," she said in a soft voice.

Lark nodded, before realizing she couldn't see him. "Yeah, that's me."

"You have your one secure?" she asked.

He looked over at her, pleased that she'd managed to clip a rope onto the other horse's halter. "Yup, let's get them over to the truck."

Lark whispered to the horse, reaching for the third one as it came closer. He now led two of them, and he wanted to get them out of harm's way as soon as he could. He hated leaving the loose horse out on the road where she could get hurt.

"Back to whether you do this kind of thing in the dark often…"

He laughed this time, shaking off the grump he'd been in since he'd found the horses in such awful conditions.

"Let's just say that I'm not good at tucking up in my own bed at night during a storm, without knowing the animals around me have the same comforts."

"Well, when you put it like that," she said thoughtfully.

Flashing lights interrupted them.

Bloody hell.

He'd hoped to resolve the situation before the police arrived. Hoped to have fled the scene. The last thing he needed was to get in trouble with the law.

Lark continued walking as though he hadn't even noticed

the approaching vehicle, taking the frightened horses over to his truck.

Thankfully they loaded easily enough. Someone must have trained them before they'd been left to their own devices. Just as they'd hoped, the other mare wandered close.

"I'll take her," he told the woman, reaching for the horse and running a hand down the mare's neck to soothe her. "Maybe you could go and stall the police for a moment?"

"Sure thing," she said, almost invisible in the dark now. "You finish up here and I'll let them know what's happening."

Lark stifled another groan. How the hell was he going to talk his way out of this one?

In his younger days, he might have jumped in the truck cab and taken off in hopes of outrunning trouble.

But he was no longer that boy who didn't want to face any consequences. He was a man with responsibilities now.

He managed to secure the other horse, now waiting to join her friends, before loading her and pushing the button to close the ramp at the back of the truck.

"Sir?"

Just in time.

Lark forced his shoulders to relax and turned. Slowly. Feet moving in a half circle to confront the male voice he didn't recognize.

"Sophie here tells me the situation is now under control."

Sophie, huh? He looked at the woman standing beside the officer. He wished he hadn't snapped at her earlier. But being beyond cold, almost getting run over and dealing with the rogue horses had been too much to handle. Especially after the year he'd already had.

What he hadn't been able to notice before was how pretty she was. What he could see of her anyway, now that she was illuminated in the police car's lights. Her hair was caught up in a high ponytail, although he couldn't quite make out what color it was, and she had a wide smile on her face despite the cold.

He felt rude that he hadn't even known her name until now.

"I've finished loading them," he responded, gesturing over his shoulder with his thumb. "I'm sorry for any inconvenience."

The officer switched on his flashlight. Lark could make out a frown on his face as the light danced in a bright arc.

"As an animal owner you have an obligation to keep them under control, to ensure they pose no threat to public safety."

Lark felt his neck hairs bristle at the condescending tone in the man's voice. They weren't even his darn horses!

He should have kept on driving. Ignored the horses. Been realistic enough to admit that they weren't his and that he couldn't save every unloved animal in the world.

But even if he'd known this was how the night would end, he probably still would have tried to help them. It wouldn't have been in him to walk away.

"I'll need to see your license, so I can make a formal report."

"Tim, I really don't think there's a problem here."

Lark didn't move. He wanted to hear what this Sophie had to say, why she was sticking up for him when he'd almost caused her to crash her vehicle. Especially after how rude he'd been.

"It looks like someone vandalized the fence, and one of the horses became stuck in it, so this man was doing his best to get the horse off the road and to safety. Right?"

Lark found himself nodding before he even realized what he was doing. "Yeah, something like that."

The officer clearly wasn't convinced. Yet. "License?" he asked again.

Lark pulled his wallet from his pocket. "Here." He passed the license over.

"International license, Mr. Anderson?"

Lark resisted being smart-mouthed. "Yes."

"Tim, let's deal with this in the morning. It's so cold," said Sophie, her voice soft.

He watched as his unlikely advocate wrapped her arms around her body, despite the thick coat she was bundled in. "I can check on the horses' welfare in the morning and report in to you then. Let's all get out of the cold."

Lark stayed silent. He wasn't about to say something and jeopardize a possible get-out-of-jail-free card.

"You sure?" the officer asked.

Sophie didn't miss a beat. "Yes, positive."

"Well, Mr. Anderson, you'll be hearing from us both tomorrow."

He had no idea what had just happened, or why this Sophie had stuck up for him. But he wasn't going to argue. If she wanted to come see the horses tomorrow he couldn't care less. So long as he could get out of his dripping-wet clothes and into something dry, he would agree to anything.

And so long as she didn't try to tell him what to do when she turned up.

"I'm at..."

Sophie interrupted before he could give her his address. "I think everyone in town knows the farm bought by the famous rodeo cowboy."

The officer had started to walk away, shoulders hunched against the wind.

Lark chuckled. "Small town, huh?"

She paused, arms still wrapped around herself. "I'll come past tomorrow and you can explain everything to me then."

"Thanks for all your help," he said, grateful at least that the night was over.

"You're welcome."

Lark watched her walk off, before springing into action himself, running back to the truck.

He'd almost forgotten about Lucy.

Damn it! So much for trying to be a good dad.

He swung open the door to the cab. "Honey, I'm so..."

Lucy was sitting cross-legged, a big smile on her face. Seeing her like that hit Lark like a swinging punch to the gut.

"It's okay, Dad. Did you get them all?"

He hauled himself up behind the steering wheel, pausing to strip off his shirt and throw it into the back in a ball.

"I got 'em honey. But I'm so sorry for leaving you in here."

She smiled like a child far beyond her years. As though she understood, as though she knew why he'd had to do it.

He felt he was making a hash of this parenting business, but she was so patient with him. Tried so hard, more like the adult than he was.

"Are we going to keep them?"

He nodded. "Yeah, I think so."

He didn't tell her that he was worried about getting into trouble. That he could be arrested or charged with theft if the officer decided to make a fuss over it.

That sometimes you had to ignore your heart and be realistic. Which was exactly what he *hadn't* done here when he'd decided to save the four horses.

Instead he reached for Lucy's hand and gave it a squeeze. He often didn't know what to say to her, how to behave or what to do, but somehow, reaching for her always made things better. It was the only thing he knew how to do.

"I…ah…I love you, Lucy." He forced the words out, even though he found it hard to admit to his feelings. The sentence choked in his throat as if it was impossibly hard to get out, as if it wasn't meant to be said out aloud. "You do know that, right?"

She pulled her seat belt on, smiling over at him. "I know."

He might not be the best father in the world, but he was trying. Hell, was he trying.

One day at a time, he reminded himself, *one day at a time.*

No one had ever said this would be easy.

Lark shut the door to the barn and braced himself for the sting of the cold. He tucked his head down and broke into a jog, ignoring the twinge in his back. Every time his right foot thumped down it sent a niggle up his spine.

He clamped his jaw tight and forced his legs to go faster.

He'd neglected Lucy enough already tonight, leaving her sitting in the truck. Even though he felt like a failure sometimes, wondering what to do and if what he did was right, he still liked to be there for her. He figured so long as she knew she wasn't alone, that he loved her, he was at least doing something right.

He kicked off his boots on the back porch and the door slammed loudly with a gust of wind behind him. Lark flicked the switch. The storm had taken the power out in the barn, but so far the house hadn't been affected. Yet.

Lark found Lucy sitting in front of the fire, the open logs burning with a steady blaze and illuminating her light blond hair like a halo around her face. She sat with a book in her lap, legs crossed, eyes down. Exactly where he'd left her.

"Hi, darlin'," he called.

Lucy looked up and gave him a smile that made his heart thud to his toes. He had loved in his life, had had his fair share of women, but the way this little girl made him feel was something else entirely. She made everything that had happened in the past year worth it, even if it hadn't seemed like it at the time.

"How's that book going?"

Lark peeled off his woolen sweater and stood watching her.

"It's good," she told him, tucking her book beneath one crossed knee. "What's for dinner?"

Oh. Dinner. He'd forgotten again.

"Um, how about spaghetti? Or maybe eggs?"

Lucy glanced up at him with a look he hoped wasn't pity.

"What about homemade mini pizzas?"

He swallowed a question mark. The last thing he wanted was to ask a seven-year-old how to make pizza. He knew everything there was to know about horse nutrition, but putting food on the table each night for the pair of them was another matter entirely.

"You know, like with the frozen bases?" she said, grinning at him. "We can put cheese and stuff on them. I can show you."

Lark laughed. What would he do without her?

"You sure you can help me?"

Lucy giggled. "Uh-huh. I do know how to cook, you know."

"Of course you do." He stifled his smile.

Lark sat her on the counter and opened the fridge, looked over his shoulder and waited for her to point out what he needed. How on earth she knew how to put food together he'd never know.

One thing he was grateful for was that though his ex-wife had been worse than him in the kitchen, they'd had a housekeeper to put most of their meals together. Maybe that's who Lucy had watched or helped.

His wife had swanned around, spent money and been thrilled with being a celebrity wife. She might not have been a bad mother, but she sure hadn't been a good one. And she'd been a pretty darn awful wife, too, come to think of it.

But it hurt, like a fist to the belly, thinking about what she'd given up. How she'd cut both of them, not just him, from her life without a backward thought. Culling him was one thing, but how a woman could give up her daughter so easily, so willingly...

Lucy gazed up at him and he gave her a wink. Forced the sadness from his face so she wouldn't ask him what was wrong.

It was just the two of them now. Plus the horses.

"You okay, kid?"

She smiled and nodded.

"You know you can tell me if something's wrong, if there's anything, you know, on your mind."

Argh. That had come out all wrong. She was seven, not seventeen. She acted so much older than her years sometimes that he forgot how little she was.

"There is *one* thing." She said the words slowly, almost cautiously.

Lark put down the knife and turned to face her.

"Okay, shoot."

"Well, there's something I'd *really* like for my birthday."

Drat, her birthday was less than a week away.

"Tell me what it is and I'll see what I can do."

He expected it to be a pile of books, the latest toy...

"I really, *really* want a puppy."

She said the words with so much conviction. A puppy? Well, he liked dogs, that wasn't a problem, but did he need something else to look after? It was hard enough looking after the two of them, the farm and keeping the household chores under control.

"A puppy," he repeated.

Lucy nodded until her head looked as though it would fall off. "Yeah, a *Labrador* puppy."

Hell, she'd clearly given this a lot of thought.

"We'll see," he said, knowing that if she wanted one that badly he was never going to be able to say no.

"Really?"

"Really."

Lucy launched into his arms and planted a wet kiss on his cheek. "You're the best dad ever!"

Lark wondered if his "We'll see" had been misheard as a yes, but he knew one thing for sure. Being the best dad ever was pretty important to him right now, so if the kid wanted a puppy, a puppy it might have to be.

He'd been floundering these past few weeks, trying his best, but wondering if he'd ever figure out how to be a good dad. Especially when he had no one to help him. And having Lucy in his arms felt so good. *Beyond good.*

Sometimes he wondered if he'd ever felt so alone. Then he'd realize how silly it was to think like that, when one look at his daughter told him they'd never be alone so long as they had each other.

CHAPTER TWO

SOPHIE dropped down a gear as her car snaked up the long driveway and approached the house. She had no idea why her stomach was fluttering and twisting, but it had been like this since she'd left the animal shelter.

She stopped outside the house and looked around. It didn't look as if anyone was home. A wide porch stretched across the front, the board siding in pristine condition, a grapevine curling its way up the main posts at each side of the entrance. A white dusting of snow was still sprinkled over the roof even though the weather had cleared overnight.

It didn't look like the home of a bachelor, but then she wasn't sure any country house would have a distinctive single-guy look.

Sophie had heard a lot about the mysterious rodeo rider who'd moved into town. She laughed to herself as she pushed open her door. She still couldn't believe she'd ended up meeting him last night and hadn't clicked the minute she'd heard his honey-laced American drawl.

Given all the gossip she'd heard about him she should have realized immediately, but then, almost running him over had temporarily scrambled her mind.

The American man with no wife that anyone had seen, who was apparently world-famous for his rodeo-riding, had all the women in town swooning. Behind closed doors anyway.

He'd looked handsome the night before, she wasn't denying that, but she wasn't sure he warranted quite that much of a fuss. Although it had been almost dark…

Sophie ran her hands down her jeans, knotted the scarf hanging around her neck and made for the door. She was about to knock when she spotted a huge barn tucked around the back.

Bingo.

"Hello?" Sophie called out as she walked toward the barn.

Nobody answered. She kept walking.

It was still cold, but the snow had stopped falling overnight, and after the rain they'd had since, almost all the white stuff had washed away, although the wind was still like ice brushing against her face.

"Hello?" Louder this time.

Sophie stopped as she approached the big stable block. Wow. The house might be modest, but the barn sure wasn't. The big double doors were open, pinned back, flanked by a large tree on each side.

It was nothing short of idyllic.

She decided to go in.

Sophie shoved her hands in her pockets, wishing she'd brought gloves. It was pristine, the walkway freshly swept, and…

She wasn't alone.

Sophie stopped. Her boots thudded to a halt and wouldn't move.

Maybe she'd hit her head during her sudden stop.

In the daylight, he lived up to every snippet of hyped-up gossip she'd heard whispered about him.

Oh, my.

He was leaning into a stall, one knee pressed into the timber frame, the other leg spread out behind him. Both his arms were crossed against the top of the door, his chin resting on shirt-clad forearms.

Wow.

Now that she could see him more clearly she realized he had to be at least six foot three, maybe taller if those long jeans-covered legs were anything to go by. His hair was dark and slightly messy, as though he'd just trawled his fingers through it.

And if she wasn't mistaken, he was talking to his horse.

A chestnut nose with a streak of white peeked out from above the stable door, nudging at his shoulder. He laughed at the horse, so softly that she only just heard it.

And then he turned.

Oh.

Dark brown eyes met hers, open and smiling, but his expression disappeared, as if he was embarrassed to have been found talking to the animal.

He cleared his throat and straightened, smiling, but his face was slightly guarded, not the same as it had been before he'd known she was there.

"Hi," he called out. His long legs hardly moved, yet the distance between them closed within a second.

Sophie remembered to smile. It shouldn't have been that hard, given the subject in front of her, but for some reason she was having a tough time remembering even to breathe. Let alone answer back.

"Morning," she replied, trying to keep her voice light and breezy, and feeling anything but.

He held out his hand to her. "We didn't really meet properly last night."

Sophie felt her shoulders relax. "No, we didn't get off to the best of starts."

She took the hand he offered, watching as his palm covered hers, its warmth taking the chill from her own freezing-cold skin.

"I'm Sophie, Sophie Baxter," she said.

"Lark Anderson," he replied, before rubbing her hand with his other palm, his mouth lifting in a smile. "And you have mighty cold fingers."

She felt heat crawl across her skin as she met his gaze. Lark just grinned at her and rubbed both his hands over her one cold paw for a moment.

"I'm sorry about, well, snapping at you like I did last night." He looked embarrassed, as though he wasn't used to apologizing. "I was annoyed and cold, and I shouldn't have taken it out on you."

Sophie tried not to become paralyzed. Something about this guy was making her brain and her body refuse to respond. At least at the same time. Somehow, she'd failed to see, to feel, his presence last night.

Granted, it had been dark, he'd been rude and she'd been freezing cold, but still. How had she missed *this?*

"So, where are the horses?" She looked down the row of stalls.

He stood back, thumbs looped into his jeans, leaning back on his heels. "There's one thing I don't understand," he said, not answering her question.

She tilted her head, unsure what he was getting at.

"When you sweet-talked the officer last night, why did he agree to you checking on the horses?"

"I'm with the local animal shelter, so he would have called one of us in anyway, and I've known him since I was a kid," she told him. "I spoke to him this morning, and he wanted me to report back to him. But…"

He took a step forward. "What?"

"He's on his way here shortly, so I'm hoping you don't have anything to, well, to hide." She had this funny feeling that she hadn't just happened upon a guy trying to load his own horses on a truck. She'd wondered about it all night.

Lark smiled at her. A lazy, out-the-side-of-his-mouth, as-if-he-was-about-to-laugh kind of smile.

"What exactly are you asking me, Sophie?"

She flushed, embarrassed. But she was here to do her job. Not get all red-faced over a man. Not now, not here.

"It's just—" she looked down at the horse with his nose still peeping over the stall, anything to avoid those deep, dark eyes watching her "—I can't quite figure out why you were there at that time of night with your horse truck." She paused, but she'd regained her confidence. This time she looked directly at him when she spoke. "They were *your* horses, right?"

"Nope." Lark walked around her and moved down the barn.

She followed him, rushing to keep up with his long strides. Sophie shook her head, wishing she hadn't become involved. She could see this was going to be one of *those* situations.

"I think you should start from the beginning," she suggested. "Please tell me I'm not involved in some sort of a crime, not after I stuck up for you out there last night."

Sophie had no idea what had happened, or how the new guy in town had ended up with a bunch of horses that didn't belong to him in the worst snap of weather they'd had in years. But it didn't feel right.

Lark stopped and turned to face her. Made her feel like the only person in the world as his chocolate-brown eyes softened. But she didn't miss the cheeky upturn of his mouth.

As her mother would have said, if it looks like trouble and smells like trouble…

"There is a slight problem," he said, "with how they came to be in my possession."

Oh, no. Definitely trouble.

Her role was to make an initial assessment, decide on a course of action. She didn't need to deal with additional problems. Especially not when she could be implicated for aiding him.

Sophie waited for Lark to explain himself.

"I uplifted them from where they were being neglected."

Oh, my.

"You stole them!" She gasped. "And I *helped* you to steal them!"

She glared at him. At least he had the decency to look at his feet, boots scuffing at the ground. But he was still smiling when he looked up. Chastised but not easily beaten.

This was going from bad to worse. And fast. Sophie felt her head starting to spin.

"I don't know if *stole* would be the most accurate word." He gave her another smile, as if it would help to soften the blow. "It was about to start snowing again when I passed them, they were bone-thin, with no shelter or feed, and one was injured badly from the wire being tangled around her leg, so I took my horse truck back and brought them home with me." He paused, serious now. "That's when you found me—and helped me."

Sophie shut her eyes for a brief second and took a deep breath. If she'd been on her own she would have pinched the bridge of her nose.

"Lark, I don't know what you'd call it in America, but I can tell you for sure that here we call that theft." She sighed. "In other words you *did* steal them."

He shook his head, and she could see the stubbornness in his eyes. She had a feeling that no matter what she said to him, he'd disagree until she saw things his way.

He'd swear to her that something was black when her own eyes could see clearly it was blue.

But he didn't argue with her. Instead he placed his hand to the small of her back and propelled her forward, warming her with his touch and giving her no other option but to move.

"I did what I had to do, Sophie." His voice was soft, but she couldn't *not* hear him. "Once you see them in the daylight I think you'll understand."

She shook her head but kept walking anyway. She was here now, and it was her job to assess the situation and figure out what to do. All she had to do was make a call on what course of action needed to be taken.

Sophie swallowed away the word *job* and focused instead on the hand resting against the small of her back. She could have quickened her pace, sped up one step, and his hand would have fallen away, but she liked the distraction.

Any little thing that took her mind off the job she *should* be doing, the career she'd run away from, was worth it. Cases like this kept her busy and stopped her from being sucked back into the past.

Lark let his hand drift from Sophie's back as they reached the gate. He made himself take a step to the side, away from her, so he wasn't crowding her space.

But not before he gave her one last quick, sideways glance. She looked troubled, as if something was on her mind, although it didn't distract from her looks. Looks that were different from what he was used to, but she was pretty nonetheless. She was like a colorful wildflower rather than the over-manicured roses he was normally surrounded by, and it was refreshing. Different in a way that took him pleasantly by surprise.

She had a mane of dark blond, slightly curly hair tied in a high ponytail, falling almost halfway down her back. Her stance was strong, confident, her brows pulled together in concern as she watched the horses.

"Come on, girls!" Lark called out and moved to open the gate.

He beckoned for Sophie to follow.

"Are they all mares?"

Lark nodded. "Yeah, but it gets worse. I'm pretty sure two of them are in foal, and the third one is only young. Maybe a yearling. It's hard to tell because she's so small. I've got the injured one in a stall."

He watched as Sophie's eyes narrowed, her face saying it all as one of the mares turned to face them. The horse's hollow expression and lackluster eyes gave away her life story. Her feet were turned up at the edges, they had been left unattended for so long; her coat was so dull it nearly broke Lark's heart.

"I'm not going to take their blankets off to show you their condition. It's too cold and it took me long enough to get the darn things on them yesterday."

Sophie looked at him then back at the horses. They were standing within a few feet of them now.

"The vet's on his way too, so we'll make sure they're all tended to."

Lark nodded. "And your friend with the law isn't going to be enlightened about what happened, is he?"

He watched her face as it flickered with indecision. Lark could tell she was torn between doing the right thing and turning a blind eye.

"I don't know what I can tell you, Lark," she said, looking from him to the horses. "I can't lie and say they're yours. It's not worth it, and he'll only figure it out anyway. Plus I'd only get into trouble myself."

He crossed his arms over his chest. Trusting a woman didn't come naturally to him anymore, but he was at her mercy. Although he liked the fact that she was conflicted over what to do. "But?"

She twirled a strand of hair between her fingers, as if she was lost in thought. "Let's see what I can do, okay? Sometimes owners of neglected animals surrender them without too much of a fuss, but then again, normally an animal shelter is the one to seize them." Sophie paused, before making her point. "Rather than an individual."

He grimaced. Maybe the smart thing to do would have been to call it in. Let someone else deal with it. But then he'd never been the sort of guy to go home to his own warm bed while animals were left out in the cold. Neglected.

"I appreciate all the help you can give me, Sophie," he told her, lowering his voice, knowing she was on the verge of deciding whether or not to assist him. "I did this for the right reasons, you can see that for yourself."

She sighed. He watched as her face softened, chest rising then falling.

"Can I ask you a question?"

"Sure," she said.

"You still call it theft?"

She gave him a sad smile. "Yeah, it's still theft, but I'm not saying I don't get why you did it."

Lark grinned back at her. "Call me crazy, but I couldn't just leave them. Not with backbones sticking out so much you could hold them like handles, or wormy pregnant bellies that would break any horse lover's heart."

Sophie paused to look back over her shoulder before following him through the gate.

"You know, I thought rodeo riders didn't give a toss about animal welfare."

He shut the gate and stopped, crossing his arms over his chest. That was something he hated—presumptions about the kind of person he was, the kind of animal-owner he was, just because of his profession. His sport. He felt his imaginary hackles rising. "I guess you've never met the right kind of rodeo rider."

Lark could have sworn he saw her blush, but she just smiled and placed her hands on her hips before giving him a business-like nod and squaring her shoulders.

"Seriously, my best horses were treated like royalty," he told her. "They only had to perform eight, maybe nine times a year, and I loved every one of them."

He felt a familiar pang just talking about his past. His former profession. He missed the rodeo circuit the way he'd miss a limb torn from his body. He'd played that scene from his last championship rodeo over and over in his mind as if in doing so he could change what had happened.

Lark looked up as he heard her sigh. "They're here."

He leaned back against the post-and-rail fence as two unfamiliar cars splashed mud up the drive, sneaking a sideways glance at Sophie. She took him by surprise, that was for sure. She wasn't the type of woman he was used to admiring. And he wasn't intending on being attracted to any kind of woman anytime soon.

But then maybe that's why he liked her.

Because the kind of woman he was used to being attracted to, to liking, sure hadn't worked out for him in the past.

Maybe her turning up and nearly running him over had been for the best last night. Without her help, he might be facing a larger problem than he'd bargained for with the local officer. And here was to hoping she still felt like sticking up for him when it came to the crunch.

He groaned, watching the cars approach.

If only he could learn to look the other way and keep driving, he wouldn't end up in this kind of situation.

Thank goodness Lucy was back at school. He didn't want his little girl to see him questioned by police. Not ever.

Sophie fought the urge to look back over her shoulder as she walked down the drive to meet the other men. She could feel Lark's eyes on her back.

Maybe the reports hadn't been false. Lark was easily as interesting as the gossip mill had suggested. Tall, dark, handsome, caring…

The only false report was that he was probably heavy-handed with his animals, given his past career.

She shook her head. No use thinking about him. It must be the cold getting to her. She was not the kind of girl to get all hot under the collar over a guy, although it didn't mean she wasn't allowed to look.

And the way he'd just taken those horses? Okay, so she wasn't going to condone his actions, but the man had guts. He was prepared to end up in a power-load of trouble because he cared too much to keep driving past neglected animals.

That gave him a definite tick in the good-guy stakes.

CHAPTER THREE

"Mr. Anderson."

Lark nodded as his name was said.

"To what do I owe this honor?" Lark tried not to sound too condescending. He knew damn well what this visit was about.

He only hoped he wasn't in too deep.

Sophie had looked dubious when he'd told her how he'd come into possession of the horses, but not necessarily judgmental. Even if she had bluntly told him it was theft. But part of him hoped she hadn't changed her mind completely, that she was still on his side.

He wasn't so sure now, but it would sure change *his* mind about the pretty blonde if she turned on him.

The last thing he needed was to jeopardize his role as Lucy's sole caregiver.

Even if he hadn't moved them halfway across the world, he'd still have no one. It was him and his daughter and no one else.

The officer glared at him, gave him a look he didn't like. Sophie smiled.

"Lark, I'm going to take some notes, record what you have to say and keep an account of the animals. And Tim," Sophie paused, "I mean, Officer Brown, wants to interview you."

Sophie smiled at him as the second man emerged from his car.

"That's the vet we work with at the shelter. He's going to assess the horses and give us any assistance we need."

She looked flushed, pink-cheeked from being busy, eyes bright, the kind of woman who didn't mind getting dirt beneath her fingernails or having to work a full day out in the open.

Lark hated that he was drawn to her, attracted to her in some way. But then maybe it was because she was so different from his ex-wife. No hair spray held each strand of hair in check, no caked-on makeup or false eyelashes batting at him. Just a real girl out to do her job.

"So this vet's going to help us?"

"He'll be establishing whether there is a definite case of neglect," stated Officer Brown.

Lark swallowed the words held tight in his throat. The bark he wanted to belt out at this imbecile. It didn't take an expert to declare there was neglect. It was fairly obvious.

"Should I take you to the house or do you want to question me here?" asked Lark, trying to sound friendly and knowing he was failing badly.

Sophie moved closer and nudged him sharply in the side. He bit the inside of his lip.

"Play nice," she whispered.

He swallowed another response, this one more like a growl. But for some reason he didn't want to upset her. Didn't want to annoy her.

"Let's get this over with, then," he muttered.

Lark watched as Sophie gave him a look, the kind of look a woman gives you when she doesn't want to be crossed. He obeyed, happy to oblige, *for now.* Only because he was still hoping he'd been right about her genuinely wanting to help.

But he did react to the look she gave the vet. He watched as Sophie turned, a smile lighting her face as the other man emerged from a dusty four-wheel drive.

It made his back prickle, as if he had spikes covering his spine.

He wasn't usually prone to jealousy, but the smile on Sophie's face was making his chest constrict. For a reason he couldn't identify, the thought of her being fond of the man, heaven forbid intimate with him, was tying him in knots.

Lark took a step back, needing distance from her.

He didn't need to be distracted by her. Not when he was a single father, not when he had to put his daughter first.

He caught Sophie's eye as she looked his way, smiling at him and playing with her ponytail as if she might have been nervous.

Even if she was cute as hell, even if there was something different about her that was starting to appeal to him, women were off his radar. For good.

They had to be.

He cringed.

A deep voice jolted him from his thoughts.

"Come on, Mr. Anderson. Let's see what the situation is here, before I decide whether to arrest you."

Sophie tried to keep her eyes on the horses. It wasn't easy, looking at animals that had been so blatantly neglected, but it was the distraction beside her that was proving to be the problem.

She'd thought about Lark plenty overnight. As the rain had pounded on the roof when she'd first gone to bed, and then as the sun had shone across her face and woken her early this morning.

There was something about him, something she couldn't put her finger on, that had her thinking. Interested almost.

Or not.

Argh. She didn't know, or perhaps just didn't want to admit, that she maybe liked this guy for some reason, even though he was causing her more trouble than he was possibly worth. But she had a soft spot for him after what he'd done.

"So you think it's fair to say that they've been like this a long time?" Officer Brown asked.

Sophie scribbled in her notebook, remembering that she was meant to be taking notes.

"Gee, you think?" Lark muttered.

She threw him a tight smile. She got where he was coming from. Any fool could see the condition the animals were in, but his sarcasm wasn't going to help the situation.

"Lark, do you want to take a walk?" she suggested.

He looked back at her. She could see he was angry by the red flush that was creeping up his neck and the steely fix of his jaw.

She gave him her most pleading look.

"Please?"

He nodded, but not before scowling at the two men standing by the horses.

"We need to let them do their job," she told him in a low voice.

Lark turned thunder-filled eyes toward her. She gulped. Angry Lark looked a whole lot more masculine, more intimidating, than smiling Lark.

"I don't have a problem with the vet trying to do his job," he told her. "Or you."

Sophie reached for Lark's arm, let her hand hover for a heartbeat, then dropped it to cover his shirt-clad skin. The fabric was soft beneath her touch, his body warmth radiating through.

She guessed he was getting hot from frustration.

"Lark, you need to be patient."

He looked in the other direction as they moved, making a grunting noise deep in his throat. But he didn't shrug her hand off, and she didn't volunteer to move it. Instead she increased the pressure, trying to ignore how strong his forearm felt beneath her fingers. Trying to infuse calmness through her touch.

He stopped when she did. Turned his big frame to face her, towering above her, something else she wasn't used to.

"Look, I'm trying to help you out here, but you're not exactly making things easy." She sighed. "If you want me to deal with this, then you need to do your bit, too."

Lark's stance relaxed. She watched as his eyes softened and the hard set of his jaw was replaced by a small smile.

He let out a breath.

"You say you're still going to help me?"

Sophie let go of his arm, suddenly feeling vulnerable maintaining contact with him like that now the moment had passed.

"In case you haven't noticed, that's what I've been trying to do."

The muscles in Lark's face relaxed. He folded his arms over his chest.

"I've been rude again, haven't I?"

Sophie felt the blush hit her cheeks before she could think about hiding it. When she wasn't hiding from her regular life she was a practicing surgeon, confident and strong, but he had her acting like a shy schoolgirl!

"Yeah."

He shook his head, slowly. "Okay, well, I'm sorry again. Maybe next time we meet I can try *not* to do anything I'll need to apologize for."

"Leave it to me, okay? I have a plan."

Lark laughed and turned back toward where they'd come from.

"I'm glad you've got one, because I sure don't."

Sophie was still flustered, but she followed him, trying to keep up with his long, loping strides as they made their way back to the horses.

"I think maybe we need to start over," he told her.

"You haven't been that bad."

"Still, next time I see you I'll be better behaved. So long as I do get to see you again?" he asked.

Sophie nodded, not sure what to say or how to respond.

Had she been single for so long that she'd forgotten how to enjoy casual banter with a man? Something told her that if that little embarrassment hadn't been flirting, then it was tee-tering dangerously close to the line.

Or maybe she was completely off and he was only being friendly.

She admired him from her vantage point, slightly behind him. He was tall but strong-looking, not lanky, the way she'd expected a rodeo rider to be. His shoulders were broad, his hair thick, his jeans snug to his hips.

Sophie hurried to keep up with him. She did *not* want to be caught checking him out, no matter how good the view was.

He glanced at her and gave her that kindhearted smile she'd already grown to like, even though she'd only seen it a hand-ful of times so far.

"Lark, I meant to say that I really admire what you did. Rescuing these horses," she told him.

His steps slowed. This time a smile turned the corners of his mouth.

"Even after your big-as-boots talk about my committing theft earlier?"

She laughed. She couldn't help it. "Granted, I was a bit too high-and-mighty with my morals."

"A bit?" He gave her a nudge in the side, his elbow gently prodding her arm.

Sophie tried to fight the flush in her cheeks again, but she doubted it worked. Her skin still felt burning hot from his at-tention.

"Okay, a lot too opinionated." She held up her hand, not letting him interrupt. "But…"

He rolled his eyes. "Why do women always have a 'but'?"

Now she glared at him. "*But* it was still stealing, and you could still get in serious trouble for it."

"But you think it was heroic, right?"

She sped up again and overtook him, not even prepared to engage. Heroic?

"Arrogant, perhaps." She threw the words over her shoulder.

Sophie refused to acknowledge his gentle chuckle. He'd gone from endearing to annoying in less than a heartbeat.

But she wasn't going to deny it felt good. A moment of flirting with a handsome man wasn't exactly unenjoyable. And it had sure taken her mind off her troubles.

Lark kept his head down. It was the only way he could deal with being a grown man getting a telling-off.

"It was irresponsible, and I'm not ruling out the possibility of criminal charges…"

"Tim, let's be realistic here," Sophie interrupted.

Lark didn't find it easy, but he kept his mouth shut. Tight. He wasn't used to anyone sticking up for him, especially not a woman.

He'd seriously underestimated her.

Maybe he needed to stop judging people so quickly.

He tried to wipe the grin off his face.

"If he stole these horses, I'm not prepared to turn a blind eye. That sort of behavior isn't acceptable here."

"With all due respect…"

Lark felt a throbbing in his temple, a pounding in his head as Sophie placed a hand firmly on his arm to stop him from continuing.

What was this idiot implying?

"Why don't we compromise here?" she suggested, giving Lark a warning look.

He wanted to growl, to put his hand on her shoulder and order this guy off his property. But he wasn't going to lose his cool, and he didn't want to get all protective over Sophie.

She wasn't his to get protective over.

"What if I agree to come here every day and check on their recovery?"

She what?

"Are you sure?" he blurted.

No. No, that wasn't going to work at all. He'd been a horseman for years. He was *not* going to have someone looking over his shoulder and telling him what to do.

Sophie turned toward him, smiling. Her eyes were kind, soft, as if she genuinely cared, wanted to help.

He tried to smile back, not wanting to alert the officer to there being a problem. He wasn't going to fight this, not right now, but seriously?

"Of course," Sophie assured him.

Lark looked away. Even though the last thing he wanted was to be babysat, he wouldn't mind seeing her again—under different circumstances.

Something about her was pulling him in, drawing him closer to her. But he didn't want to be indebted to anyone, didn't like anyone doing him favors.

He didn't have the strength or desire to become close to another female other than his daughter. Not now, and maybe not ever.

The officer was still standing, not talking, one hand rubbing back and forward across his chin.

"If I agree to this, it will be your responsibility to ensure they are not moved from this property, and that they continue to receive the treatment they require."

Sophie nodded. Lark just looked between them. He couldn't believe this woman was prepared to help him. He was grateful, sure, but this was not what he wanted.

"Will you agree not to press charges?" Sophie asked.

And she was a negotiator, too. Who would have guessed?

Lark resisted the urge to put his arm around her. At least she'd got this goon off his back.

"If we find the owner, and he or she agrees to surrender them…" Lark found himself holding his breath as Officer Brown delivered his verdict. "Then, yes, I'll give my word that charges will not be laid."

"Won't you be looking to charge the *owner?*" Lark felt like a kettle about to boil over. Did this idiot not realize that he wasn't the criminal here?

"You're treading on very thin ice, Mr. Anderson. You should be grateful Sophie's decided to assist."

Lark wanted to snap, to react, but he resisted. Even if it felt like stopping a cat from catching a mouse.

Sure, he was grateful, but...

Sophie walked toward the officer, holding out her hand.

"Deal. I'll come here daily and report back to you."

Lark watched as the deal was sealed, before Sophie turned back to him.

He didn't bother to say goodbye to Officer Brown

"You think you can put up with me for a while?" she asked.

Lark pushed his hands into his jeans pockets. "I don't think you'll be that hard to have around." She wouldn't be, so long as she wasn't going to be looking over his shoulder all the time.

Sophie smiled, playing with her hair. She'd gone from stoic negotiator to sweet, pretty woman all over again.

"Do you want a cup of coffee before you go?" He asked her before he'd even thought it through.

Lucy was at school, so he didn't have to worry about her for another few hours. And besides, he liked to be sure about someone before he introduced them to his little girl.

He and Lucy had both been hurt too often only to get close to another person, trust them and then be let down again. Even if it was someone who was just a friend they'd only see once in a while, he was protective. He couldn't help it.

"Sure, why not?" she replied.

Lark made a gesture with his arm, indicating toward the house.

He could thank her for her help, then persuade her that daily visits to check in on him weren't really necessary.

Or something like that.

CHAPTER FOUR

LARK stood awkwardly in his own kitchen. He placed his hands on the counter for something to do with them.

He liked that Sophie was smiling. He hadn't liked the frown on her face, the downturn of her mouth, when she'd chastised him for his attitude. Or given him *that look* that told him he was treading on thin ice with the vet.

Not that he should care. But he did.

"So, why aren't you still riding broncs in America?"

Lark laughed. "Broncs, eh?"

It felt like a long time since he'd been able to sit and relax, to chat with another adult. Especially a woman. And it was nice. Even if he was reluctant to admit it.

But talking about what he'd left behind was never going to be easy.

"Isn't that what you call those crazy horses over there?"

"My last ride was at the championships in Las Vegas," he told her, making himself go back in time. Wanting to talk about it but at the same time not. "I wouldn't have retired if I hadn't had to, but I was told that one more concussion, another big fall, would be the end of me."

He didn't tell her that the reason he feared for his safety and life was because of his daughter. He wasn't ready to go there yet. Was too protective over Lucy even to want to introduce her to anyone new.

"So you had to walk away from it?"

He nodded sadly. "I was defending my championship titles, and I didn't even leave the ring conscious."

Sophie gave him a big grin. "But you're okay, so that's what matters, right?"

Yeah. More than she could ever know.

"And you? Have you lived here all your life?" he asked her. Lark cocked an eyebrow. He saw her hesitate, watched her almost flinch before she planted a smile on her face to answer him.

"I grew up here, but I've recently returned." She paused, before standing and putting her coffee mug in the sink. "And now I'd best be off, lots more to do today."

Lark thought he'd hit a sore point and wondered why she didn't want to talk about herself. But it wasn't as though he was keen on baring his own soul. Talking about how his career had ended had been hard enough.

"Well, I guess I'll see you tomorrow, then?"

And he guessed that now wasn't the best time to tell her she needn't drop in each day.

Sophie wrapped one arm around herself, trying not to stare at Lark. She was feeling off balance, unsure of herself. Standing here in his kitchen, chatting about why he'd come here, she was so curious she could burst.

Something about the guy had piqued her interest, and she was finding it hard not to show her feelings. The last thing she needed was the complication of getting involved with a man, and she wasn't even sure this particular man was interested.

One minute he looked at her as though he liked what he saw, or at least that's what she hoped she recognized in his eyes, and the next he seemed to back off. Big-time.

"Does the afternoon suit tomorrow?"

Lark gave her a lazy smile as he rinsed out their coffee mugs. "Sure thing."

Sophie returned his smile. It was comfortable being with him, but at the same time it wasn't. There was something she couldn't put her finger on. But she wasn't ready to open up to an almost-stranger and tell him her life story or why she'd come back.

"Thanks again for, you know, helping me out like you did," he said.

She kept walking, not looking over her shoulder at him. Not letting herself.

He was too close for comfort. Especially because she was starting to feel more for him than a stirring of attraction. The last thing she wanted was to become lost in those deep brown eyes.

"Don't worry about walking me out," she told him.

She heard Lark's footfalls stop behind her. She did a half spin on her heels, having the confidence to face him now she knew there was distance stretching between them.

"You'll be okay with the horses until tomorrow, then?"

He leaned on the doorjamb. "Yeah, I'll be just fine."

She wanted an excuse to stay longer, to talk to him, to spend the day in his company. She didn't know why, but something about him was drawing her in, making her want to be with him for as many minutes, hours, as possible.

Still, she had to go. Didn't *want* to be pulled further toward him, when she already felt as if a propeller was trying to blow her straight back to his kitchen for another cup of coffee.

She swallowed.

Or across the veranda and into his arms.

The last thing she needed was to think about those golden, muscled arms or the breadth of his chest.

"So, you're, um, clear about what meds the horses are to be given?"

Lark watched Sophie. She was standing with one hand on her hip, the other shielding her eyes. Her face was serious. Part of him wanted to tease her, play with her, make her pillowy lips turn into a smile. But the other, more sensible side of him? That told him he'd teased enough earlier, before they'd come inside.

Teased enough for a man who had no intention of taking things any further, that was.

And he didn't. No matter how cute she was.

The last thing he wanted was to lead her on.

"You don't need to worry, Sophie," he said, trying his hardest not to mock her. "I've cared for a few horses in my time."

She flushed. Lark fought not to laugh. He hadn't met a grown woman in a long time who actually, genuinely blushed. In California, in the circles he mixed in, the women had been bold and brazen. They knew what they wanted and nothing seemed to embarrass them. Ever.

This girl? She was something else.

He just couldn't put his finger on what the something was, and why he was feeling that it was something he should be interested in.

"I don't mean to belittle you, I'm…"

He shrugged, finishing her sentence. "Doing your job. I know."

Sophie tugged at her ponytail as if she was nervous. "Until tomorrow, then."

She turned to walk back to her car, but not before looking back one last time.

"You sure you're happy to care for them? I mean, to take on the responsibility?"

"Maybe it will give me a better standing with the police. Might keep them off my back for good," he said, hoping he sounded convincing.

She looked sympathetic, mouth pursed. "We'll do our best at the shelter to have the animals surrendered into our care, Lark. I'm sure there won't be a problem."

"All you can do is your best."

She gave him a wave, ponytail swinging from across her shoulder to hang down her back.

"See you tomorrow."

Lark would have watched Sophie go, would have struggled to take his eyes from her, but his phone started bleeping. The sharp ringtone took him by surprise. He fished it out of his pocket, glancing at the screen as Sophie opened the door to her car.

Oh, crap.

His ex-wife.

She only ever called when it had something to do with money, never to ask about Lucy.

He'd gotten over his marriage falling apart pretty quickly once he'd realized that his wife had only ever been there for the money and the fame that came with his world status on the rodeo circuit. Once the parties and endorsement deals were over, so was their marriage.

He looked back down the drive, to where Sophie's car had not long disappeared.

If there was one thing his ex-wife was good at, it was reminding him why he was single.

And right now, he had no intention of changing that. Even for an entirely different woman in an entirely different country.

Even for a sweet-natured, pretty girl named Sophie.

CHAPTER FIVE

LARK grinned at his daughter as she excitedly recounted the tales of her day. He couldn't help it. Just being with her reminded him why everything hard in his life was worth it. Something had changed within him when he'd taken over sole custody of Lucy, and it was for the better. Nothing else seemed to matter quite so much as hanging out with her.

He took his eyes off the road for a split second to catch a glimpse of Lucy again. She had the window half-down, face turned toward the breeze, loose strands of hair whipping around her cheeks.

"So what else happened? Did you learn anything?" he asked her.

She wriggled back to face him. "Of course!"

"What kind of stuff?"

Lucy played with her hair. "I don't know, but we did lots."

He chuckled.

"Oh, there was one thing," she said.

Lark raised an eyebrow and glanced over at her. "What was that?"

"I asked my teacher about the Fourth of July, because you know how it's next week? And she said that no one here does anything to celebrate it. Or Thanksgiving."

Of course. He'd forgotten all about it.

"Did she explain to you why it's not celebrated here?"

Lucy nodded. "She said that Christmas is the big celebration here, but that Thanksgiving and the Fourth of July were only important for Americans."

Lark leaned back in his seat, one hand on the wheel. He wasn't quite sure what Lucy was getting at, but he had a feeling she expected him to come up with something.

"If we were back home in California, what would we be doing to celebrate?" he asked her.

Lucy looked thoughtful. She had her bottom lip caught between her teeth. "Um, we'd have fireworks I guess, a barbecue, and we'd all hang out together."

Okay, so he definitely had to do something about the Fourth of July.

"But," she said, "it would be really hot, not freezing cold!"

He laughed. "Well, I can't do much about the weather. I think the hot dogs would freeze on the grill if we tried to have a barbecue out in the snow! And the horses might be frightened by the fireworks."

"Oh." Lucy's face fell. "I guess you're right. Does that mean we won't have Thanksgiving, either?"

Darn, Lark hated to let her down. After the past year of upheaval, he only wanted his precious daughter to be happy in her new home. How would she feel about giving up Thanksgiving and the Fourth of July, which had always been big events back home?

"Hey, maybe we could switch them around a bit?"

Lark had to smother a chuckle at the way Lucy's eyes lit up with hope. She had a child's trusting innocence.

"We could have a log fire and a turkey on the Fourth of July, when it's cold outside, and a barbecue and fireworks in November, when it will be hot again. We'll go to the far paddock, away from the horses, so they won't be scared."

Lucy bounced up and down enthusiastically in her seat. "Cool." Her eyes shone with glee.

Yeah, cool, Lark thought. He struggled enough with day-to-day meals, now he had to figure out a turkey dinner. In July!

"But would it only be the two of us?"

Lark shrugged. "Maybe. Let's see if there's anyone else we want to invite closer to the time."

Lucy sat back in her seat, looking out the window again.

The Fourth of July. Funny, it had been such a big part of his life, traditions like that, for so long, and now it was no more than a distant memory.

"You know, last Fourth of July I had dinner with you then went off to the championships in Las Vegas," he told Lucy.

Only to fall and finish my career forever.

Now he was thinking about doing a dinner from scratch himself, for the two of them. No rodeo, no drama, just their little family of two.

"Are you going to ride rodeo again?"

Lucy had her head on an angle, like a puppy waiting for a command.

"No, honey," he said. "Any riding I do will be at home or with you."

That made her grin. "If I had a *pony* you mean."

"Be patient, miss. All good things come in time."

She rolled her eyes like a teenager before catching his eye and laughing.

It was at that moment that Lark knew exactly where he'd rather be. What life he'd rather be living. Even if he did have to deal with a back that still hurt like hell sometimes. And questions about why Mommy no longer wanted to be in their lives.

Especially in moments like this, when everything felt so easy. So happy. So effortless.

Lark reached out for Lucy's hand, her tiny palm slotting in against his. She hadn't even turned from looking out at the fields whizzing past, but her little hand was warm, feeling out for his the moment he reached for it.

If this wasn't love, he didn't know what was.

Sophie parked her car and walked around the back of Lark's house. She didn't bother knocking on the door. He'd be out with his horses or working the land; there was no chance he'd be inside.

She was looking forward to seeing him. He was different from the men she usually met. The kind of successful guys that were used to women swooning, impressed with them being surgeons or specialists. Besides, most of the men she met these days were already happily married.

Lark was different. For starters, he didn't even know she was a successful pediatric surgeon. As far as he knew, she was a nice local girl who worked at an animal shelter. And she liked that. Sometimes her training intimidated men who weren't in the same kind of career, although she doubted it would faze Lark. But she liked that with him she didn't have to be that woman.

Sophie looked up as she heard the sound of a horse moving across the ground, hooves rhythmically thumping.

Lark was working a horse in a round pen. He was standing in the centre, the horse moving around him. She walked slowly over to the edge of the corral, resting one foot on the bottom rail and leaning against the timber.

Wow.

Lark was impressive to watch. He was tall, especially with a cowboy hat on his head. His posture was relaxed, voice soft as he spoke commands to the beautiful big animal moving gracefully around in circles.

At his command, the horse slowed to a walk and came in toward him. It stopped a few steps away, blowing softly from the nostrils, and Lark reached out a hand to stroke its beautiful chestnut head.

Then he moved toward the horse's shoulder and gracefully vaulted onto its back.

She'd never seen anything like it.

No saddle. No bridle on the horse's head. Nothing.

Just Lark, speaking softly, riding bareback, the horse moving to his commands. He was completely in control despite having no gear on the animal.

"Hi."

Sophie looked around, the soft, high-pitched voice surprising her.

Oh.

A young girl stood not far from her, leaning against the corral, a messy blond pigtail over each shoulder and a shy smile on her face.

"Hi," Sophie said back.

The girl let the fingers of one hand trail along the timber as she walked slowly around the edge of the round pen. It gave Sophie a moment to calm herself, to deal with her thoughts.

Who was this child? And what was she doing here?

"I'm Lucy," the girl said.

Sophie tried not to notice the resemblance to the patient she'd lost before moving back here. The girl who had died on her operating table before she'd taken her extended period of leave.

"Sophie," she said back, wishing the ground would open up and swallow her.

Once upon a time she would have loved nothing more than to chat to a child. Now? It filled her with terror. Because it only reminded her of what she'd lost, and what she now knew she'd never have herself.

"He's a very good rider, isn't he?"

Sophie didn't know what else to say.

Lucy nodded. "Yeah, he's the best."

She looked from the girl to Lark, wishing he'd stop riding and save her from this conversation, or that she could simply disappear back the way she'd come.

"Ah, why are you here on your own, Lucy? Are your parents nearby?"

That made the girl laugh. "I'm here with my dad."

"Where is he?"

Lucy scrunched up her face, squinting into the afternoon sun.

"*He's* my dad."

Sophie looked to where she was pointing. Lark was now trotting around in a big circle, seemingly oblivious to the conversation that was going on.

She looked back at the child.

Surely not? Lark was a...*dad?*

Lucy had moved closer to her, was leaning on the fence beside her, so close they were almost touching.

"Are you okay?"

Sophie made her head nod up and down. She was in shock. Seriously?

"What about your mom?"

The child's face lost its perky smile.

"No, it's just me and dad."

Phew. Even though it was awful this child didn't have a mother here, Sophie would have felt terrible for having flirted with someone else's husband. For having the kind of thoughts she'd had about Lark earlier.

Him having a daughter made things tricky enough. She didn't have the heart or strength to be around a child. Not right now.

"Do you know my dad?"

Sophie tried to encourage her tongue to work properly, her mouth to roll around the words she was trying to form.

"I'm...ah, well." She took a deep breath. "I'm here to help your, ah, *dad* with the horses he rescued the other night."

Lucy grinned up at her. "Oh, yeah, I know who you are."

If she could have made the ground open up and swallow her she would have, instead she leaned against the timber railing, focused on Lark rather than his child.

"I'm going back to the barn now," Lucy announced. "See you later."

Sophie gave her a smile and raised her hand. Speechless.

Because that tiny child had promptly reminded her of what she'd never have.

Sophie swallowed the lump in her throat, forcing the

thoughts away. This was not the time or place to start choking up.

"Hey."

Sophie jumped at Lark's voice.

"Hi," she replied.

He moved the horse closer to her.

"I see you've met Lucy."

Sophie nodded. "Uh-huh."

"Hope she didn't talk your ear off."

Sophie didn't meet his eyes. Couldn't. Because suddenly she had guilt twinging in her belly, twisting her insides, at the thought of being even *mildly* attracted to someone's daddy.

She fought in her mind for something to say, anything other than talking about the child.

"I hope I wasn't interrupting, walking over like that to watch you."

He gave her a lazy smile out one side of his mouth. "Nope."

"You're impressive, I'll give you that."

A lightness lifted her shoulders. She had to ignore his daughter. She was here as a professional, nothing else.

There was nothing wrong with observing, with sharing a laugh with him and checking in on the horses. She just had to leave any romantic notions in her head. Or forget about them altogether.

"It's what I do." He gave her a casual shrug.

"It might be what you do, Lark, but from down here it's pretty impressive."

"Do you want to watch while I finish up with Cougar, or are you in a hurry?"

She looked over her shoulder. Lucy was no where to be seen.

"Cougar?" she asked.

Lark nodded, dropping a hand to rub over the horse's neck. "He's my boy. Came with me all the way from California. I've had him since he was a baby."

That figured. They looked in tune enough to read one another's thoughts.

"Maybe for a few minutes. Then you can take me over to check the others."

Lark indicated with his head toward the entrance of the corral. "Come on in. You can stand in the middle and I'll talk you through what I'm doing, if you're interested?"

Sophie brushed her hands off on her jeans and gave him a quick glance before moving around to the gate. She was interested in watching him, to take her mind off things. Until it wasn't just the two of them anymore and then she'd leave. As soon as his daughter returned she was out of here.

"Sure," she said cautiously.

Lark waited until she was in the corral, standing in the center, then he started moving the horse around her.

She was fascinated. He was so controlled, so gentle in his movements, and the horse was so relaxed beneath him.

It cleared her mind of everything.

He was mesmerizing.

"You see how I'm using my inside leg?" Lark spoke softly, his eyes never leaving the animal.

"What does that mean?"

Lark glanced at her, and then she watched as he applied pressure with the other leg.

"He moves away from my leg, that's how I tell him which direction to go in."

The horse started to trot then, making Sophie turn faster to watch them.

"Now I'm squeezing with my leg to ask him to move faster." They broke into a canter, moving faster yet again. "And now I'll ask him with my body to slow down."

Sophie twirled around to watch them. Fascinated.

Then she saw a grimace flash across Lark's face.

He brought the horse back to a walk. Fast.

Was he in pain? It had only been a burst of something, a

reaction, but she knew pain when she saw it. It was what she dealt with on a daily basis.

"You okay?"

Lark smiled, but she could tell he was bluffing. It didn't hit his eyes.

"Fine. Why wouldn't I be?"

She frowned. "I thought something happened up there."

Lark shrugged off her question as he would a fly landing on his shoulder. "I'm fine. Just an old twinge."

Sophie pursed her lips, desperate to examine him. To run her fingers over the spot that pained him and see if there was something she could do to help, even though it wasn't her area of expertise. But to do so would mean she'd have to explain... And that was not something she wanted to do.

Not right now.

Lark brought Cougar into the center to stand a few paces back from her.

"Are you sure you're okay?" she persisted. "I don't mind taking a look if you're, ah, sore or anything."

He looked at her quizzically, and she could almost hear his question. *What could you do to help?* He looked a little annoyed, although he was trying hard not to let it show.

"Show's over," he said, dismounting, boots hitting the ground with a soft thud.

She wondered if maybe he'd pushed himself too far, if it was something to do with his old injury. He had said a fall had ended his career.

But she was too chicken to ask. She had to try to forget who she was, ignore her medical training and not read so much into every situation.

"Can you do that with any other horses?"

He grinned—that sideways, sloping smile that made his eyes crinkle at the edges. As though he'd forgotten all about what had troubled him earlier.

"It takes time, but most horses can be restarted to respond in the same way." He stroked his horse's neck, fingers gently thrumming back and forward. "Cougar and I have been working together a long time, but for a stallion he's incredibly respectful."

Sophie's fingers were itching to touch the horse's silky chestnut coat herself, but she refrained. Doing so would mean moving closer to Lark, and she didn't need to be any nearer to him.

The look of him alone was enough to send her mind and heart racing, especially after seeing the way he was with his horse. Being around him was exciting, infectious, intoxicating.

And being this close to him all of a sudden made her forget all about the pain she'd seen on his face earlier. Right now he looked happy and…more than a little enticing.

She gulped. She'd also forgotten, for more than a moment, that he had a child.

"Shall we head back in?"

Sophie hoped he couldn't read minds. "After you."

Lark didn't want to look at her. Or want to be with her. Or anything else romantic.

But for some reason his eyes were drawn to Sophie and he was finding it darn hard to pull them away. Even the horse nudging him in the side for attention wasn't helping any.

He couldn't help but see the humor in the situation though. After years of rodeo-riding and putting more than a few noses of those who didn't agree with the sport out of joint, here he was getting friendly with an animal-shelter worker.

Lark laughed to himself. The animal advocate and the cowboy. Not something he'd ever thought could even happen, and now he was tripping over himself to impress her.

"Before, when you asked me about my back, how did you know I was in pain?" He had to ask her, it was bugging him.

Sophie looked guilty. Or maybe he was imagining it.

"Just a hunch." She said each word in a slow, deliberate way. "I thought you looked like something was hurting you."

Huh. He thought he'd done a good job of working through the ache in his back before. He might have pushed himself too far, *again,* but he was doing better than he had been last week. Or the week before that.

"So it's been all quiet on the law-enforcement front today?" Sophie asked him.

"There's been no word from our good friend Officer Brown, if that's what you're thinking."

Sophie looked over at him and smiled. He wondered what she was thinking. Whether she'd thought about him in the same way he'd started to think about her.

Ridiculous, when he hardly knew her, but still. Maybe he was lonely, maybe he was just on the rebound after what his wife had done to him.

Or maybe he actually really liked this girl, which was why he was finding it so hard to tell himself to stay away from her.

"You really care about them, don't you?"

He ran a hand down Cougar's neck as they neared the stable block.

"You mean the ones I rescued?"

Sophie moved her head slowly back and forth, disagreeing with him. "No, I mean all of them." She paused and let him pass, so he could tie Cougar up outside his stall. "The way you are with them tells me you actually love them. I can see it in the way you touch them."

Lark nodded. She was right, he did.

Other men he'd met during his career couldn't have cared less about the horses they rode, or the bulls they climbed aboard, but he'd never been like that.

"The work I did doesn't mean I did it without a conscience."

Sophie gave him a funny look. She pursed her lips then sighed.

"I don't mean to judge, it's only I didn't expect you to be so…"

He chuckled. "So what?"

"Nice, I guess."

That silenced him. If he'd been looking her in the eye when she'd said it he might have even blushed.

Lark didn't know when he'd ever had another human being say something so genuinely kind to him. Out of the blue like that.

He picked up a brush to give Cougar a quick rubdown before putting him back in his stall. Sophie was looking around, hands in her pockets.

As though she was nervous.

"You want to help me?"

She stopped fidgeting. "Ah, sure. But you'll have to show me what to do."

Lark bent and reached for another two brushes, holding them up. "You see this one with the firm bristles? It's a dandy brush."

Sophie moved closer to inspect and Lark didn't move out of her way. He stood still, hoping she'd move closer.

"You use this on the sweat marks."

She reached for the brush, fingers skimming his as she took it from him. Lark kept his eyes on the brush, on her hand. He didn't see if she did the same.

"Like this?"

He raised his gaze as her body moved sideways, watched her run the brush over Cougar's coat.

"Yeah, like that," he said, hearing a gruff note to his voice.

She turned back, eyes on his. This time Lark didn't fight it, didn't look away.

"And that one?"

He held up the other brush, before holding it out to her.

"It's soft," she said, running her fingers across it.

Lark took a step in toward her, this time not scared of the proximity. He wanted to touch her, to see if the thoughts in his head were worthy of tormenting him.

"Lark—"

Lucy's pretty face and windswept blond hair suddenly appeared beside them, and Sophie's voice cut off so instantly it was as if she'd been choked.

He didn't have time to turn and look at Sophie. Lucy was bouncing around, vying for his attention.

"Hey, honey."

She grinned and gave him a wave, before skipping over.

"Whatcha doing?" she asked, eyes focused behind him on Sophie.

Lark turned, surprised to see the frozen look on Sophie's face. The start of a smile was locked on her lips, her eyes were wide, and she wasn't moving.

Weird.

"Lucy, you did introduce yourself before, didn't you?"

His daughter nodded enthusiastically. Sophie still stared.

"Hi," Lucy said politely.

Oh, boy. Sophie's head started to pound all over again, little red spots playing in blotches before her eyes.

Her heart somehow rose to touch her tongue then thudded all the way to her toes.

His pretty blonde and blue-eyed girl stood before her, lips pulled back in the widest smile Sophie had ever seen, eyes dancing.

Waiting for Sophie to talk back to her. Anything other than staring at her as if she had two heads.

It was stupid. So he was a parent? Why was it affecting her so badly?

"I've moved the horses a few fields over if you want to take the truck down to them."

Sophie's mouth was dry.

She needed to check the horses, fast, then leave.

Because she couldn't deal with this. Not now. *This was what she'd run away from.* Having to deal with situations like this.

She couldn't face up to little people. Especially not little ones who were the same age as the child she'd lost on her table. And the child she'd voluntarily dismissed all those years ago.

The child growing in her belly that she'd decided not to keep.

"Sophie?"

She looked up, trying to shake off the stunned expression she knew would be taking over her face.

"Sorry, I…" she took a deep breath. "I think it's time I had a quick look at those horses and then let you two get back to your afternoon."

Lucy was still grinning at her. Lark looked unsure.

Sophie knew she had to snap out of it. Fast.

"Why don't we all jump in the truck and go see the horses?" Lark was speaking to his daughter, too.

Lucy nodded.

No. She did not want to be stuck in a confined space with a child and her father. Especially not this particular father. Being witness to a display of happy families was not what she needed.

"I, ah, should really be off," she started to say, not sure what excuse she could come up with.

Lark frowned slightly, his brows meeting as if he was deep in thought.

"You're not interrupting, if that's what you're worried about."

Sophie shook her head. She tried to make the movement subtle, even though she could easily have shaken the darn thing off.

"Really, Lark, I'll take a quick look at them on my way out then get going."

Lark raised an eyebrow, before giving her a tight smile. "Okay, we'll take a rain check."

She watched as Lark dropped a hand to his daughter's head, giving her fluffy blond hair a ruffle.

Sophie swallowed. Gulped. Almost choking on her own saliva.

How had she gone from feeling so relaxed, so *comfortable* around Lark, to wanting so badly to escape?

But she knew. Goodness, did she know.

Seeing Lark like that with his daughter…it reminded her of what she couldn't have.

She could never have children of her own, and that wasn't something she could ever imagine coming to terms with. Not while her heart was beating could she comprehend a life that wouldn't include a child in her future.

CHAPTER SIX

SOPHIE ran her hands over the horse's coat before standing back. It had taken a lot of guts for her to turn up today. She'd been tempted to try to pass the case over to someone else at the shelter. But she never shirked her responsibilities, and there was something about Lark that kept drawing her back, something that compelled her.

But now that she'd been confronted with his daughter again, she'd decided any future visits would be within school hours.

Avoidance she was good at. Dealing with issues—not so much. She'd held it together enough to keep her composure, now that she'd had time to process the fact that Lark was a dad, but it still wasn't easy.

"You're doing well, Lark."

He leaned back, his shoulders braced by the timber stable framing. "I do know what I'm doing," he said drily.

But Sophie could see the glint of a smile behind his sarcasm.

She looked up when she heard a shuffle and saw Lucy skipping toward them again. Not looking at them, lost in her own world.

Sophie couldn't help but ask about her. For some reason she had to know more about her, even though it hurt. More than she could describe.

"Your little girl, she's about seven or eight?" she asked.

Lark followed her eyes, looking where she looked. "Yeah, about to turn seven."

Sophie took a deep breath, hoping she wasn't asking too much. Wouldn't be seen to be probing.

But she had to know.

"And it's just the two of you, right?"

Lark's face darkened. Like a storm cloud ripening over the planes of his cheeks, his eyes and across his mouth.

"Yes. Just the two of us," he said firmly.

Sophie wished a hole would open up and swallow her. "I'm sorry, I…"

He pushed off from the stable door. "No need to apologize," he told her. "I'm hoping we're better off just the two of us, given what happened back home." He paused. "But that's a story for another day."

Sophie patted the horse's neck again before stepping from the stall.

"I didn't mean to pry—but I wondered if she'd lost her mom."

Sophie loved her own mother, couldn't imagine not having her in her life, but she did know what it was like to have only one parent.

And it made her curious.

Even if she did find it hard looking at the child without feeling a pang for what she'd lost herself.

"Let's just say that Lucy's mother had more important things in her life than being a mom."

What? "Sorry. I thought she must have passed away, not…"

He sighed. "Sometimes I think it might have been easier if she *had* passed away. Well, easier on Lucy anyway."

"She *gave her up?*"

Lark smiled sadly. "Yeah, something like that."

Sophie watched the girl play, getting closer to them now.

She knew only too well what it was like to have a parent walk away. It had happened to her. Not as a little girl, as an older girl, but it had hurt all the same.

But still, she didn't want to get involved here. Even thinking about children was hard for her right now. She didn't have
the strength.

"You know, call me naive, but I thought the bond a mother
had with her child would run deeper. You know?" he said, his
face a combination of anger and sadness. "I thought it would
have been too hard to walk away."

Sophie gulped. What would he think if she told him what
she'd done? That she'd fallen pregnant and given up her child?
Did it matter that she'd regretted it almost every day since?
Did that make her decision any more forgivable?

"I'm not trying to make excuses for her, Lark, but she must
have had her reasons."

He looked angry now, brows drawn together in a furious
line.

"There is no excuse for what she did," he said, voice thun-
derous. "I don't care that she left me, or that she wanted out of
our marriage. But look at that child. *Look,*" he commanded.

Sophie followed his gaze, trying to stop the sting of tears
as they threatened at the back of her eyes.

"You tell me how *anyone* could walk away from that child."

His voice was low, soft now. Sophie couldn't look at him.
Didn't want to. Because the compassion and love in his words
had stirred an emotion in her that she wanted so badly to ignore.

"I'm sorry, Sophie." Lark's voice was still raw. "I didn't
mean to get all heavy, it's…"

She waited, blinking away tears before turning to him.

"I love her so much, and I want to do everything I can for
her. I only wish I didn't have to try to explain to her why her
mother doesn't want to see her anymore."

"I wish I knew what to say, Lark, but I don't," she said.
"From what I can see you're a great dad. It's all you can do."

She knew from experience that she was right. That one
great parent was better than two unhappy parents.

Lark looked down, scuffed one boot into the sawdust below.

"Coming here was tough, but it was the right thing." His voice was soft as his eyes met hers. "We're going to be okay here. I know it."

Sophie's whole body softened.

She hadn't been wrong in her feelings for Lark. He was a kind man, to horses and obviously to children, too.

It had been something that had always been important to her, always been a quality she'd wished for in a man. But now it was irrelevant. She couldn't have children of her own, would never plan a future and a family with a husband.

And that's why being around Lark and his daughter was tough on her.

Lark swallowed; there was a knot in his throat. He had no idea what it was about this woman, but he'd opened up to her in a way he hadn't in a long while.

He'd only admitted what had happened, hadn't even gone into detail. But since Kate had walked away from him and Lucy, the only person he'd really told, really described the reality to, was his lawyer.

Kate hadn't wanted him or their daughter, and he'd finally said it out loud to another person. She'd dismissed them from her life like unwanted baggage.

And the weird thing was that the look that had crossed Sophie's face, the flicker in her eyes, had made him wonder if on some level she understood.

"Do you have children?"

Sophie looked alarmed. "Me? No."

He had a feeling he'd hit a nerve there.

"I'd better be off now," she told him. "I'm already running behind."

Lark wished he hadn't asked her that question.

He watched as Sophie looked at Lucy, before letting out a shallow sigh and collecting her bag from where she'd dropped it.

He wasn't sure what was going on, what had rattled her, but

he had a feeling it had something to do with Lucy. Or what he'd told her.

It had to.

"So you'll be back tomorrow, then?"

She turned sadness-tinged eyes toward him. "Of course."

"You know, you don't have to keep checking up on me." He wasn't sure if it was the right time to tell her that he didn't want to be babysat, that it was grating him that he had to have a supervisor. Even if she was good company.

"Lark, I gave my word that I would."

He sighed, stretching out against the timber fence. "All I'm trying to say is that I know what I'm doing here. I don't need anyone telling me what to do."

Sophie gave him a happy look, but he felt it might have been forced. "If you want a different supervisor, all you have to do is say."

Lark touched a hand to her back, wanting to guide her out, but she jumped. Alarmed.

Although she did turn, eyes tracing his in a sad arc.

"I don't want another supervisor, Sophie. I'm not used to being babysat." There, he'd said it.

She pursed her lips. "You know what you're doing, I get that. But I'm not going back on my word. And besides, you could still get in big trouble."

Fine. He'd said his piece, he didn't want to argue.

Besides, spending time with her wasn't exactly difficult.

"See you tomorrow, then."

He let his hands fall to his sides as she said goodbye. He wished he was still touching her, that his hand was still covering the bare skin of her arm.

Because he liked her. No matter what he told himself, he did like her. And the feel of her skin against his felt good. Better than good, it felt *right*.

Lucy bounded up beside him, catching the fingers of his right hand and tucking herself against him. It caught him by surprise, made his thoughts switch in an instant from Sophie to his girl.

He loved that Lucy could be so kind and affectionate to him, when sometimes he felt like such a failure. When he struggled to know how to be a great dad.

But he saw that same look cross Sophie's face as he pulled his daughter toward him. That same look he'd seen before.

"Bye, Lucy," she said.

Lark watched Sophie go, his arm still looped around his little girl.

And then he realized what that look was.

It was a look he was sure he'd sported on his own face time and time again of late. And it was a look he'd seen on his daughter's face, too.

Sophie was hurt.

It showed in her eyes, in her smile and in her voice.

Anger bubbled in his throat, through his muscles. Made him feel protective, like a grizzly bear over cubs.

He wanted to know what had hurt her, because if she'd been hurt anything like he had, he knew she would be burning, feeling ripped apart inside.

The weird part was he felt it had something to do with Lucy. That his daughter had upset her. It should have made him want to push Sophie away, because he didn't want to get involved with anyone, and he certainly didn't want to spend time with someone who didn't like children. But then he wasn't sure if that was even the problem.

Lucy tugged on his hand. "Can we go feed the horses now?"

He bent and dropped a kiss to the top of her head. "Sure can, kiddo. Let's go."

CHAPTER SEVEN

SOPHIE was starting to feel as if she'd spent more time at Lark's place than anywhere else lately. Silly, but she was stressing herself out over visiting him too often, even though she was under orders to do so. But he *had* indicated that he didn't like her looking over his shoulder.

She walked around the rear of the barn, almost hoping she wouldn't bump into him at all. After seeing Lucy the other day, the conversation they'd had…she gulped.

Who was she kidding? What she couldn't get out of her head were the tiny pinpricks of excitement that had hovered over her skin when Lark had touched her. The tingle she'd felt when his eyes had looked so deeply into hers that her breath had been stolen away.

Sophie's heart landed in her toes before climbing back up to its rightful place in her chest. That was how she felt every time she'd thought about Lark since yesterday.

But then she'd remember Lucy. And it would leave her empty.

Confused. Unhappy. Lost.

How was it that the one man she was mildly attracted to, the *only* man she'd even considered romantically in far too long, had a child? The one thing she was running from.

Sophie sighed. Part of her wished she hadn't had to come here today. But then she knew, deep down, that she was lying to herself. Not coming here would have made her even more miserable.

She shook away the thoughts that were a constant burden on her body, niggling at her, and leaned on the fence to watch the horses. There was nothing for her to freak out about. She didn't need to let anything happen between her and Lark, and she could just come during school hours if she didn't want to be around his daughter.

The stupid thing was that she wasn't even needed here and they both knew it, but the shelter wanted the logbook filled in every day in accordance with police orders. And she'd volunteered for it, after all.

Sophie hitched one foot up on the rail, and watched the horses she was supposed to be keeping an eye on. The sun was shining today, and Lark had taken their blankets off. Their coats were still pretty lifeless, but already their ribs seemed less obvious and they looked happy enough.

The sound of a throat being cleared made Sophie startle. Anticipation fired heat into her belly, and she felt her skin flush, like warm honey being drizzled over ice cream. Telling herself that Lark meant nothing to her was starting to sound ridiculous, even in her own head.

Sophie turned, and…

"Tim?"

She frowned. What was he doing here?

"That would be Officer Brown to you." He said the words with a smile, but she could see more than a hint of seriousness on his face.

Sophie hadn't called the police, which made her wonder if… Surely he wasn't here to arrest Lark?

She mustered up a smile and walked closer to Tim, prepared to stick up for her new friend.

"What are you doing here?" Sophie asked in her cheeriest voice.

He tipped back his hat slightly. "Checking up on things,"

he said, before looking around. "And with a message for Mr. Anderson."

Sophie's heart started to beat faster again. Surely he wasn't going to press charges?

"Did you manage to track down the owner of these poor horses?" she asked.

Tim gave her a look that said it wasn't her business. But it was. She was here every day sticking to her end of the bargain, so she deserved to know.

"I'd prefer to speak to Anderson in the first instance."

Sophie shook her head, willing Lark to appear. Why was Tim being so formal about the matter? "He might be on the property, but I haven't seen him yet."

Tim walked closer to her, then passed her to look into the field, watching the horses she'd only moments before been looking at herself.

"Sophie, you're not covering anything up here, are you? Sticking up for this guy when you shouldn't be?"

Damn it. Why was everyone so wary of new residents? Just because he hadn't been living here long didn't make Lark any less trustworthy than the locals. It was times like this she preferred her city life.

Sophie tried not to appear too angry. "Look…"

"To what do I owe this pleasure?"

Sophie almost shut her eyes with relief as Lark's deep drawl rang out from behind her.

She watched as Tim turned to assess the cowboy standing to her rear. Lark covered the ground with determination until he stood beside her.

"I've been in touch with the owner of the horses," Tim said, not even looking at Sophie.

The steel-like brace to Lark's stance worried her. He had his hackles up and it didn't look as if he was going to be very good at hiding them, and what they all needed to do right now was stay calm.

"I don't believe for a moment that your intention wasn't to

steal those horses, and I'm not convinced Sophie wasn't involved from the beginning, but you can count yourself lucky that the owner doesn't want to press charges. Which means I'll keep my word on not arresting you for theft."

Now Lark was glowering. Sophie bit her bottom lip. He looked like a stubborn, arrogant cowboy, the type she doubted would back down. Sophie just hoped he'd keep his mouth shut long enough for them to hear the rest of what the cop had to say.

"But you'll be charging him with neglect, right?" asked Lark, his tone even.

Tim took a few steps forward, but Lark kept his arms folded, not budging an inch.

Damn it. He clearly wasn't good at keeping his mouth shut after all.

"You should be counting yourself lucky that you're not going to be spending the night in the cells. You stole his animals, and we're fortunate he's prepared to surrender them and not pursue criminal charges against you."

Sophie moved forward, resisted putting a hand on Lark's arm to calm him and smiled sweetly at the two men.

"The animal shelter can still pursue the case, though, right? I mean, that's what we do."

Lark had anger rippling like bolts of electric energy through his veins. He could feel the tick of annoyance bulging near his cheek, and it took every inch of his willpower not to clench his fists.

Or smack this uptight cop in the face.

He tried to exhale some of his anger. Thinking like that wasn't going to help him. And neither was Sophie stepping in and trying to stick up for him, even if she was only trying to help.

"Look here," said the officer, face burning red with anger. "There's a rumor around town that our newest local has a reputation for being a troublemaker, so don't think you getting away with this means I won't be keeping a careful eye on you. And don't even think about telling me how to do my job, or who I should or should not be arresting."

Lark forced himself to calm down. This guy didn't have a leg to stand on, and he had no intention of even being within a step of trouble again. Well, not if he could help it.

"I can assure you, *Officer,* that I'm not a troublemaker, and I have no intention of being a problem in town or anywhere else for that matter."

Sophie looked on edge, angry.

"Really, Tim, I can't believe you'd listen to idle gossip."

Lark turned to look at Sophie as she spoke the same time the cop did. Only, he was trying to stifle a smile and this Tim guy was looking like thunder warmed up.

"It was nice to see you again, Sophie. Mr. Anderson, I'll be back if I have any formal complaints about your behavior."

Lark stood still, refolded his arms and scowled as the officer walked back around the front of the property and headed for his patrol car.

He only changed his stance when he saw the droop of Sophie's shoulders.

He walked up behind her, crossing the grass to where she'd moved to, and touched her shoulders. One hand on each shoulder blade, fingers curling down slightly onto her upper arms.

"You okay?" His voice came out low, softer than he'd expected.

She only nodded in return.

For a moment he wondered if she'd lean back into him, but she just stood, not moving away, not giving in to his touch.

Lark swallowed. And again.

He didn't want anything to happen, not really, but he wouldn't have pushed her away if it had.

He appreciated her standing up for him, that was all. *Surely that was all?*

"Do you know what that was really about?" he asked.

Sophie moved away from him, then turned around.

"That's why I don't like small towns sometimes."

He laughed, relieved that she was smiling again. "You telling me that's the kind of thing I have to get used to putting up with here?"

She leaned back against the fence. "I hope I didn't make things worse for you. I probably should have kept my mouth shut."

"It's my own fault, not yours, so don't go getting worried about it," he told her. "I'm lucky you stood up for me that night."

He watched as Sophie shut her eyes, rubbed at the bridge of her nose then gave an exhausted sigh. He didn't care about the cop turning up—he could deal with that—but he didn't like seeing her rattled. She still had that slightly unsettled look on her face that she'd had the day before when she'd left.

"You sure you're okay?"

She nodded. "Yeah, I'll be fine."

He was still trying to figure out what had upset her about seeing Lucy—it was slowly gnawing away at him—but he didn't ask her. Wasn't his place to. And he wasn't the kind to pry.

"I'll deal with him if he becomes a problem, Lark. In fact I plan on kicking up a stink if something isn't done about the owner being prosecuted." She gave him a smile, a real one, not like the tight smile she'd forced at the officer before.

Good. He didn't need any trouble, no matter how tempting it would be to have it out with the cop.

"I guess I owe you, then?"

She shook her head, ponytail bouncing back and forth. "Not a chance. You did a good thing here, and besides," she said, her smile suddenly shy, "it wasn't theft if the intention was right, huh?"

Lark grinned. Well, when she said it like that...

"How about a tour of the farm? Since you had to leave in such a hurry yesterday before we got a chance."

Sophie looked panicked for a moment, but he watched as

she carefully composed herself. Something was definitely troubling her. Something bubbling away beneath the surface that he couldn't put his finger on.

But the moment passed, and she tilted her head, eyes smiling at him. "Sure," she said, after only the briefest of hesitations.

"Horseback or truck?"

That made her shake her head, fast. "It's been a while since I've sat astride a horse."

She fell into step beside him. "So you used to ride?" he asked.

"More like I rode the odd pony at a friend's place. I can stay on, but that's about all. Nothing serious."

"I thought with you working at the animal shelter that you…"

She interrupted him. "Are we going to tour the whole farm?"

Lark guessed she was trying to steer clear of talking about herself. Suited him fine, he wasn't going to push it. He wasn't exactly one to open up his soul on his own background.

"There's a track around all the flat ground, but we'll stay clear of the hills. I don't fancy getting out to push if we get stuck at this time of year."

He gestured toward his truck with his thumb, and watched as she moved around to the passenger side.

He was on dangerous territory here and he knew it.

The sensible thing would have been to keep his distance. Instead he'd come up with a way to spend more time with her. He'd figured out how to get her alone, to be in close quarters with her when what he should have done was stay as far away from temptation as possible.

His heart thudded as he realized that she was probably under no obligation to visit him anymore. That she might not be coming over daily now, or even ever again if he didn't ask her to.

And no matter what he told himself, he liked her, even if women were meant to be off his radar. To think that only yesterday he'd been all high-and-mighty and told her that he didn't want her checking up on him and those darn horses.

Lark watched her as she glanced shyly down at her feet, hiding her hazel-brown eyes. The way she tucked a strand of fallen hair back over her ear.

There was something almost sad about her smile sometimes, as though she was holding something back, but he didn't care.

Lark pulled open the door and got in beside her, inhaling the faint aroma of her perfume as he sat close.

"There's not really that much to see," he told her, almost apologetically.

Sophie leaned back in the seat, turned her head to face him and smiled. The same kind of smile that he thought said she was hiding some sort of sadness.

"It's just nice to be here. Doing something different."

Lark focused on driving. His mouth was starting to feel a little dry.

Because the more time he spent with this girl, the harder it was to convince himself that he should remain celibate.

Sophie wasn't sure if she was comfortable being in the cab with Lark or not. The space felt too intimate, which was stupid. She'd traveled with plenty of people in cars and never felt like this before. But there was something about the man, his presence, that made her jumpy. On edge.

That made her feel as though she needed to wind down the window and let the sting of winter air hit her cheeks, or fling the door open and make a run for it. Just to have space to breathe, to stop thinking about how attracted she was to him.

But she didn't. Couldn't.

Something was telling her she had to stay, that she was meant to be here and that something had pulled her in this direction for a reason.

Even if that did sound stupid.

"What made you move here, of all places?" The question burst from her mouth before she could stop it.

The way Lark's jaw hardened, visible from his side-on profile, told her she should have kept quiet.

"Ah, well, it's a long story."

In other words he would rather jump from the moving vehicle than talk about it.

"Sorry, Lark, I shouldn't have asked."

He shrugged, the tightness in his face disappearing.

"It's okay." He paused.

Sophie wasn't going to make the mistake of asking again. She didn't want to talk about why *she* was here. It had been unfair to spring that on him.

"You must be pretty passionate about your horses though. And it's a great place to set up a horse stud."

That made him smile. He threw a grin her way. "If there's one thing I'm going to do here, it's make a name for myself with sport horses."

She laughed. "As opposed to getting up to mischief and having the locals gossiping about you."

The space between them felt calm again, lighter. As though they were friends taking a relaxing drive on a Sunday afternoon.

"Sophie, I know you don't celebrate the Fourth of July here, or Thanksgiving for that matter, but I was wondering…"

She found herself holding her breath. Wondering what?

He looked almost nervous, even though she could only see his side profile. "Well, it's just I was thinking of doing a Fourth of July celebration, and I thought maybe you'd like to join us."

Sophie knew the sensible answer would have been *no.* But sensible fled her brain when she looked at Lark. She saw the worry lines on his face, indicating it was a big deal to have asked her. And something told her that Lark, somehow, was good for her soul. He made her feel lighter and happier than she had in a long while.

"A Fourth of July celebration? Doesn't that involve red, white and blue flags and a picnic? Might be a little chilly!"

She knew she was stalling for time, but she needed to catch her breath.

He let out a chuckle. "We're switching the Fourth of July and Thanksgiving, so it will really be a Thanksgiving dinner—you know, with a turkey and potatoes. Inside." He wished he'd never asked. Why was he babbling? "I didn't want Lucy to miss out on our traditions from back home."

"Dinner. With the two of you?"

He threw a smile her way. "Yeah."

But it wasn't simply dinner with Lark. It would be dinner with his daughter too, and she wasn't sure she was up for that. Would it be healing or detrimental to her?

Lark seemed to sense her hesitation.

"I could be wrong here, but did Lucy say something to upset you? Was she rude when you first met her? Because I thought her manners were pretty good, but I could be wrong."

Sophie shook her head, fiercely. So he had noticed.

"Heavens, no, she seemed like a sweet child."

He kept his eyes on where they were driving. "It was just…"

She needed to nip this in the bud before he asked too many questions. Before he went where she didn't want to go.

"She reminded me of someone else, that's all. It took me by surprise."

Silence stretched between them. She hadn't exactly lied, but then she hadn't been entirely honest, either. She couldn't talk to him about the child she'd lost professionally, or the one she'd lost privately.

"So what do you say about our Thanksgiving-cum-Fourth-of-July dinner?"

Sophie was torn between wanting to make up an excuse and giving in to what she wished she could cope with. Was it stupid to feel upset about his daughter? About letting her own emotions, her personal issues, stop her from enjoying an evening in the company of a man she was attracted to?

"I'd love to." She made herself push out the words, impossible as it felt. She couldn't punish herself forever, and it meant a lot that he'd asked her.

His face relaxed. "Great. I'm sure Lucy would like some extra company. It can't be that exciting hanging out with her dad all the time."

"You seem to be doing a great job, Lark. Don't be too hard on yourself."

If there was one thing she did admire, it was a parent stepping up.

"I'm hoping so."

They both sat in silence for a heartbeat that seemed to last an age. Sophie squirmed in her seat. She needed to change the subject.

"I don't know much about Thanksgiving, come to think about it," Sophie admitted, attempting to change the subject away from parenting. "I know you eat turkey meat, and that's about it."

Lark laughed. The noise so sudden that it took her by surprise. "You know what?"

She tried not to laugh back at him. The look on his face so comical as he slowed the truck and stopped. Mood lightened.

Sophie shook her head. "What?"

"I don't really know anything about Thanksgiving dinner either, because I'm usually just the one eating it."

"At least you know *something* about it."

"Just bring yourself on the fourth and I'll do my best to show you a traditional Thanksgiving dinner. In July." Then in a softer voice, "Lucy is desperate for a proper feast, and I'll be darned if I'm not going to try."

It was as if claws had tightened their grip around Sophie's throat. *He* might not know it, but *she* knew he was a great parent. She could tell simply from the way he spoke, from the way he wanted so desperately to be there for his daughter.

"What do you want me to bring?"

"Just yourself."

The way Lark looked at her, his eyes flickering over hers

for less time than it took for her heart to somehow thud to her toes, made her think that maybe he had just asked her on a date, rather than a regular family dinner. And she'd said yes without quite realizing.

He bent closer, a fraction, and she thought he was going to kiss her. That he was moving closer for a reason. But he stopped, didn't move any more.

She wished her eyes weren't locked on his lips, looking over the fullness of them, wondering what they'd feel like on hers.

He cleared his throat, pulled back slightly.

Made her feel as though a gust of antarctic air had blown between them, chilling the burning heat that had been there only a moment before.

"Why are we stopping?" Sophie half choked out the words to change the subject, to get her mind off bringing "just herself" to dinner.

Lark opened his door then leaned back in toward her, a cheeky smile on his face.

"This is the best view of the land," he said, winking before getting out. "From lower ground, anyway."

Oh, my. Maybe she'd gotten herself in a little too deep here. The man was having a serious effect on her, even if he was someone's father and should be completely off-limits.

Sophie opened her own door and stepped out, desperate to inhale fresh country air and fill her lungs with it.

Wow.

"You know what? I grew up here, Lark, and somewhere along the way I forgot how beautiful it was."

She'd been so busy fluttering inside about the man beside her, and talking a dime to the dozen to him, that she'd failed to notice exactly where they'd been heading. She wouldn't have wanted to miss this for the world.

"If it wasn't still so wet I'd take you higher, but it's pretty nice here."

"Nice? It's incredible." Sophie sighed and leaned against the vehicle.

Neither of them said a word. Lark was propped against the front of the truck, and even his big frame couldn't distract her from the surroundings. Fields stretched out as far as she could see, houses were dotted here and there and the land was full of horses and cattle. Everything looked so green at this time of year, not dry and parched as it would be in summer.

"You talk about this place as though you spent a long time away."

Sophie froze before regaining her composure. She hadn't meant to have this conversation.

"I've, ah, not long been back here," she said, hoping the words didn't sound too stumbled. "I went away for university and to work, but now it's just nice to be home again."

She watched as he looked out over his land. "I can see why you wanted to come back."

Phew. She didn't want to get into specifics. To have to tell him that she'd left to make a difference, to become a success-ful pediatric surgeon. That she'd succeeded but then not been able to deal with the joint blows of losing a little person on the table and coming to terms with her own loss. Of finding out that no amount of loving children could ever help her, be-cause she'd never be a mother herself.

She stifled a sob that was burning to escape her throat, and forced it back down.

"I saw this place advertised on the internet, and bought it before I'd even been to see it."

Sophie was pleased he hadn't noticed her pain, wanted to keep talking about him to take the heat off her. "Had you ever even been here before?"

"To Queenstown?" he asked, raising an eyebrow and look-ing back at her. "Yeah, a long time ago. I was actually born in New Zealand. We left to go back to the States when I was three or four years old when my father's company transferred him again. For some reason it just felt right to come back here."

Words hung unsaid between them. She knew there was probably a lot he wasn't telling her, a lot still unsaid between them, but she found she didn't even want to know. Curious? *Yes.* Nosy? *Desperately.* But until she was ready to share her own reasons for coming back, she wasn't going to pry and try to get him to divulge his.

He surprised her by exhaling a lungful of air and turning to tell her more.

"I'd always dreamed of retiring here one day, but I never guessed I'd only be thirty-five when my career ended." There was what she guessed was a bitter edge to his voice. "And I never thought I'd be a solo dad."

She didn't know what to say. He probably didn't want her to say anything.

"Anyway, being here feels right. Since Lucy's mom doesn't want anything to do with her, in a way I thought it would be easier to have distance from her." He paused. "Does that sound stupid? Trying to protect her, so she doesn't realize that her mom doesn't want to see her? Giving her mom an excuse not to visit her because an ocean divides us?"

Sophie shook her head. Sadly. It wasn't fair and she knew only too well what that felt like.

"So I'm guessing they had this photo on the advertisement?" she asked, looking back out at the view and trying to change the subject. She wasn't ready to open up to Lark. Not yet. Maybe not ever.

"Yeah." Lark turned away from the view to face her. "This, the house, the town—having forty acres to call my own. Everything felt right. I don't know why."

"Have you met many people? Been shown around properly?"

Sophie didn't know why she'd asked. She was hardly the right person to introduce Lark to the locals. Not anymore.

He shrugged. "I've met a few people, but you're the first person I've actually spent any time with."

She sensed he didn't mind that. That he liked being a bit of a loner, even though she was enjoying his company just fine.

"Shall we head back? I'll drive you down past the big field then we can loop back and see the rescue horses."

Sophie followed his lead and walked the few steps back to the truck, opening the door to get in.

"I never asked you how many horses you have here."

Lark stopped, his tall frame making it easy to look at her over the roof.

"I've got my boy Cougar, who I'll be using to launch my breeding program, and a mare that I bought before I left, but I sold all the others back in California."

She noticed a wave of something cross his eyes. Sadness, she guessed. It must have been hard, whatever his reasons, to leave his four-legged friends behind. Not to mention every-thing else that he'd been through.

"Then there are a couple of mares I picked up locally. But I need to invest some time and money into finding more that will suit the type of sport horses I want to breed."

Sophie lowered herself into the truck when he did. She'd thought it before but she couldn't help thinking it again—it was nice to meet a man who was so passionate about his ani-mals.

Sometimes, especially during her short time back here, she'd started to wonder how humans could be so cruel. How some could see nothing wrong with inflicting pain on defenseless creatures. Maybe that was why she was struggling so hard with her own past.

But Lark? He was the kind of man who restored her faith in humankind.

A big, strong, strapping guy, as manly as they came, yet who wasn't afraid of being seen as softhearted when it came to his horses.

CHAPTER EIGHT

SOPHIE fought the urge to flee, but made herself ignore it. She wanted to leave so badly, but at the same time something within her didn't want to let Lark down. After what he'd told her the other day, the way he'd opened up, she was reluctant to up and leave.

Even if being around Lucy was like torture.

She wasn't sure how she was going to cope with having dinner with the pair of them this weekend, was terrified of playing happy families, but she wanted to try. There was something too magnetic about Lark to turn down dinner with him, even if it was going to test her. Push her boundaries.

Make her confront thoughts she was trying so hard to run from.

But she couldn't run from everything.

"Hi!"

Lucy burst around the corner of the stables and landed almost in front of her. Sophie smiled at the child's enthusiasm. She couldn't *not*.

And in that single moment of exuberant excitement, Sophie felt a twinge of recognition. That look on Lucy's face was why she'd become a surgeon. Why, up until now, she'd dedicated her life to saving the lives of little people.

Even if it had been hard, had pushed her to near breaking, it had been worth it.

She forced thoughts of her old job from her mind, not wanting to go back there yet. Not now.

"Hey."

Lark stepped around the corner a second after his daughter had darted into one of the empty stalls.

"I wasn't expecting you today."

Sophie smiled at Lucy's father. "I'm here to do a final report for our records," she told him. What she didn't say was that she could have done it from the office without visiting again. But she'd wanted one last excuse to turn up without having to be invited. She was going to miss this, seeing him each day. "I hope you don't mind?"

Lark shook his head slowly. As though he was considering her.

"I don't mind at all."

Lucy reappeared from the stall, pigtails flying.

"Is there anything to eat?"

Sophie stifled a laugh, surprising herself that, for a moment, she felt so relaxed around a child.

"Snack time, right?"

Lucy grinned. "Yup."

"You want to join us?" Lark asked.

She wasn't sure if she was up to spending the afternoon with the pair of them, and she did have to get going...

"Sophie?"

She snapped out of it. "I'd best be off, but I'll walk around the front with you now I'm done here."

Lucy ran ahead and Sophie fell into step beside Lark. Something about being beside him felt right, relaxed and comfortable.

"She seems to be doing okay."

Lark tilted his head, looking at her as they walked. "By okay you mean not a complete train wreck?"

His smile caught her off guard. She couldn't help but return it, even though Lucy was the last thing she wanted to discuss.

"I had a parent leave when I was a thirteen," she told him, not wanting to make the moment somber but feeling as though she had to help him. Give him at least a bit of guidance. "I, well, I guess I know what she's going through, in a way. I mean, I was old enough to grasp why he left, but it didn't make it any easier."

Lark's face went blank, then the corners of his mouth dropped.

"Your father?"

Sophie found it hard to push the words out. She didn't often talk about her father's indiscretions. Hardly talked about him at all, come to think of it.

"My dad left my mom for another woman," she told him. "His secretary, just to be a complete cliché. And my mom was left with nothing. Two kids to look after, the house with the white picket fence, but no husband, no job, nothing other than the memory of once having had the perfect family." She tried to keep the bitterness from creeping into her voice, but didn't succeed.

"I'm sorry."

She shrugged. "We were probably better off without him, but it sure didn't feel like it at the time."

"Ditto here," he said. "I hope I did the right thing, but you never know. Maybe Lucy will grow up to resent me taking her away, but all I know is that her mother has washed her hands of her, so all I can do is my best. I'll never understand her, but maybe that's a good thing."

Sophie could have cried. Hearing a father talk like that, it was, well, special. So beyond her experience to hear a dad take complete responsibility.

"She seems fine, Lark. If she's smiling every day then I don't think you have anything to worry about. One good parent is better than two average ones."

That was something she knew from experience.

They walked around the house in silence. Lucy stood on the porch waiting.

Sophie had to look away.

Just seeing that pretty, shining little face reminded her of what she'd lost. The child she should have been able to save, the child that could be waiting for her with open arms on her own porch. And the child she'd now never have.

Sophie gulped, swallowed away the emotion that was starting to pool in her throat. It crept up on her like this, took her by surprise and wrapped around her like a fist clenched around her throat.

Lark's phone ringing took her by surprise. She watched as he fished it out of his jeans pocket.

He looked at the screen, before apologizing and taking the call. "Sorry."

Sophie watched as he answered then walked a few steps away.

"You want to come inside and play?"

She turned slowly on the spot and saw Lucy standing closer to her now. One arm was curled around the veranda post, and she was leaning out as far as she could without falling.

"Ah, no, I should probably get going."

Lucy's smile deflated. "Okay."

Sophie was uncomfortable. She looked back over her shoulder at Lark. He had the phone in his hand now, call over.

"Everything all right?" she asked.

She noticed the hard line of his jaw. "Yeah. I've been trying to buy a horse for a while, and now that they've decided to sell I've suddenly got competition."

"Oh."

He shoved the phone back in his pocket. "They told me I could go look at her now and have first option, but I don't want to drag Lucy out again. She's been doing enough of that these past few weeks."

The words fled Sophie's mouth before she could retract them. "Do you want me to stay with her?"

She regretted them instantly. Hoped he'd say no.

"Would you?"

She kept her voice bright. "Of course."

"Well, if you're sure," he said, a smile spreading across his face. "I could be there and back in an hour or so."

"Go," she said, trying to sound confident, yet too scared even to turn and look at Lucy. "I'm happy to help out. We'll be fine."

"Lucy?" Lark turned to ask his daughter. "That sound okay to you?"

Sophie forced herself to turn toward the child. Raised her eyes.

"Does that mean you'll come and play now?"

"Sure," she said, waving Lark off. "But why don't we play outside? You can show me around all your hiding places."

Lucy shrugged as though she didn't mind what they did. "Can I show you my tree house?"

Sophie watched as Lark turned before walking fast into the house, presumably to get his keys. He mouthed *thank you* before disappearing.

She jumped as a tiny hand found hers. Sophie looked down, knowing it was stupid to be scared of the little girl tugging gently on her hand to hurry her along.

But she was. This was scarier to her than a pack of wild dogs snapping at her heels.

She hoped Lark didn't take too long.

Sophie climbed up the ladder behind Lucy, wondering how on earth she was going to fit in the little wooden house nestled up the tree.

She squeezed through the gap and found Lucy perched, legs crossed, waiting for her. There was more room than she'd expected.

"Wow." The view was incredible. "You can see out over all the fields."

Lucy looked proud, happiness beaming across her face. "Dad made it for me. It's my own house."

Sophie laughed. "Yeah, I guess it is your own house."

They sat there, both staring out at the view, as if they were on holiday and looking out at the ocean. Both were lost in thought. Sophie wondered what such a small girl could be thinking about.

She didn't have to wonder for long.

"Sophie, do you know why my mom didn't come here with us?"

Oh, heavens.

"I don't know your mom, honey."

Lucy sighed, sadness crossing her face, making her eyes and lips turn down at the sides. As if she didn't feel loved.

"What I mean is that I don't know your mom, but I do know your dad," Sophie corrected, scrambling to think of what to say. Of how to help her.

Pain shot through her, told her that she wasn't ready to have this kind of conversation. To get too close to Lucy.

But at the same time she knew she needed to say *something* to help the child.

"Sometimes, well, sometimes parents can't stay together because they don't make each other happy anymore."

Lucy's eyebrows rose. "Is that why Mom doesn't call me? Because I don't make her happy anymore?"

"Oh, honey, no!" Sophie shuffled closer to Lucy, put an arm around her without thinking. Comforting her as she would have done to one of her patients.

She gulped at the softness of the child against her, the sweet smell of her fluffy blond hair.

"Just because your mom and dad don't want to be together anymore doesn't mean they don't both love you. But sometimes it's okay to have only one parent." Lucy's big blue eyes looking up at her touched Sophie's soul, reached within her and tugged at her heart. "I know, because that's what happened to me."

"It did?"

Sophie knew she'd said the right thing. Lucy's voice was curious, amazed even.

"Yeah," she said, leaning and drawing Lucy back with her. "When I was a kid, a bit older than you, my dad moved away and I only had my mom."

Lucy nestled into her, tucked her warm little body against Sophie's.

She wondered if it were possible for her heart to break any more than it had already in the past few months, but it was—because being with Lucy, talking to her and being in her company, was reminding her of what she missed so much.

She'd become a doctor, a surgeon, because she wanted to help people and do something important with her life. And she'd specialized in pediatrics because she loved children and knew she could be the kind of doctor who'd connect with them.

Sophie swallowed and pressed her eyes tight shut, willing the hot, sharp burn of tears to go away. The inferno in her throat, the emotion surging through her told her it was never going to get any better. That somehow she was being punished for what had happened in her past.

"It's okay to miss your mom, but you have a dad who loves you so much, and that makes you the luckiest girl in the world."

"You want to go see the horses again?"

Sophie looked down at Lucy, pleased that she looked happy now. That she was ready to change the subject.

"Yeah, why not?"

Lucy pulled away and made for the ladder, disappearing from sight.

Sophie sat for a moment, knees drawn up close to her chin. This was why she'd been scared when she'd found out Lark was a dad, after being so attracted to him.

Because this was the life she wanted so badly, and she was only being reminded of what she couldn't have.

"You coming?" Lucy called out from below.

Sophie shuffled to the ladder and wriggled her way back down.

She already knew she liked Lark. What scared her was how quickly she could like his little girl, too.

And that was starting to sound and feel like dangerous territory.

Territory that she wasn't even remotely ready to consider.

CHAPTER NINE

LARK jumped from the car and ran up to the front door. He'd only been gone a little over an hour, had made his decision to buy the beautifully bred mare immediately, but he still felt bad.

"Lucy?"

He walked through the house, not hearing anything, then he saw them sitting outside and sipping from mugs. He opened the door and went out.

"You must be freezing out here," he said.

Sophie and Lucy both looked up as though surprised to see him standing there.

"Hot chocolate." Sophie raised her mug. "Lucy said she hates being stuck inside."

The sun was peeking over the mountain, but the wind was still icy. Lucy grinned at him over her mug.

"I'm sorry I took so long. I should have just taken Lucy with me."

Sophie shook her head. "We were fine, Lark." She paused. He watched the way she considered Lucy, the way she sighed. "I enjoyed it."

Lark looked at her, really looked at her, and found he couldn't break the gaze. Her eyes spoke of sadness and kindness, and he saw a tenderness in the way she watched Lucy that startled him.

"I'd better go."

He wished she'd stay.

"I'll see you tomorrow night though, won't I?"

She stood, casting a last glance at his daughter before rubbing her hands over her jeans and moving away.

"Of course."

He reached out to her, wanting to touch her, needing to make a connection with her.

"Thanks, Sophie. I really appreciate you helping me out here."

She looked startled, froze as his fingers skimmed hers when he withdrew his hand. But she didn't look angry.

Sophie looked as confused as he felt inside.

Lark clamped his jaw down again so hard he felt a pulse tick near his temple. He had to, to take his mind off what watching her was doing to him. What *touching* her had done to him.

He'd vowed to put his role as father first, to do nothing to compromise his relationship with Lucy.

And even thinking of being romantic with another woman was off-limits. It had to be. For now anyway.

So why was his heart still beating that bit too fast, and why was his hand clammy where he'd touched her?

And why was he looking at Sophie standing beside Lucy and thinking it looked so right?

Sophie's hands started to shake as she drove away. She felt a pull back to where she'd come from, back toward Lark, but she wasn't going to let herself be drawn in. Couldn't.

Not now. And probably not ever.

He was a father, and she didn't want to be around his daughter. Even if she did love children more than anything in the world. Because she couldn't face being hurt again.

Lark scared her, terrified her as much as he appealed to her. Because she could see that if she fell for that honey-laced drawl and those dark brown eyes, she could get completely lost. Like a car with no GPS, she'd veer in the wrong direction, lose herself head over heels, then have her heart broken into a million tiny pieces. Not to mention how hard it would be for her to get close to his daughter when she still had guilt riding heavy on her shoulders.

Which was precisely why she had to avoid anything happening between them. Keep it fun at a little flirting, if anything. Try to remember who she usually was back in her normal life. What she had to deal with in her real world. She couldn't get involved with him or Lucy.

Her problem was that something within her, some tiny niggle, kept telling her that he would be an equally fantastic lover, too. The kind of man she'd once imagined a future with.

And that, given the chance, deep down, she'd love to be close to a child like Lucy. To be there for her, give her the mother figure she so desperately craved.

She wondered if that would fill not only the void in Lucy's heart, but the one in hers, too.

Sophie's phone bleeped.

Saved by the bell. Phew. She'd had enough of *those* types of thoughts for the day. For the week, even.

"Hello?" She answered her hands-free phone.

"Sophie, it's your mother. Are you free?"

She smiled, hearing that voice through the earpiece. Good, her mother could distract her.

"I've a house call to make, then I will be."

"Why don't we have a coffee?"

That sounded perfect. Just what she needed.

"I can be at the café in an hour and a half."

Her mother hung up and Sophie turned up the radio. So long as her mom hadn't heard any gossip about her spending time with Lark from some gasbag locals, coffee would be the perfect distraction.

Funny, she thought. She'd come back home to distract herself from work and her own life problems, and now she was here she was needing distraction from a certain tall, dark and handsome cowboy. Not to mention his equally intriguing daughter.

She sighed and let her head loll deeper back into the headrest.

If only that cowboy wasn't quite so handsome, maybe she'd be able to refocus on why she was here.

But so long as she had tomorrow night to think about, there was little chance of dealing with anything else. At least for now.

"Now, I've heard a few rumors about you spending time with our resident cowboy."

Sophie wanted to drop her forehead to the table and thump it hard, over and over. She'd forgotten how fast word could travel around these parts. But seriously, how had her mother heard she'd been at Lark's place? Especially when it was only for work?

Instead of acting like a dramatic child, Sophie raised her coffee cup, took a slow sip, then looked her mother directly in the eye.

"I've been visiting his place a bit for work. Reporting on some horses he has in his care."

Her mother gave her a smile that said she wasn't convinced.

"Don't tell me he's mistreating his horses? Honestly, it's the last thing we need here."

Sophie tried her hardest not to show a hint of emotion, of anything, as she answered. "He's a good horseman. He's helping the shelter out with some neglected horses, that's all."

"And somehow you managed to wangle the job of checking in on our newest eligible bachelor?"

Her mother laughed. Sophie gritted her teeth and tried to take another gulp of coffee. *Do. not engage,* she chanted internally. Sometimes she wondered if mothers were secretly like lions or some other predator. They got a hint of blood, or in this case juicy gossip about their offspring, and they didn't back down until they'd completed the kill.

"I'm hardly on the lookout, Mom. And even if I was, I doubt I'm his type."

Now her mother was smiling—the cat-who'd-gotten-the-cream kind of smiling. "So I take it that he's every bit as handsome as the local ladies have been saying?"

Sophie only shrugged in response.

"And from your lack of conversation, I'd say he's gotten under your skin."

Argh. Seriously?

"Mother, I'm almost thirty-two years old, not eighteen, and he has *not* gotten under my skin. He's just a nice man I happen to be assigned to checking in on." She paused, glared at her mother. "That's *all*."

"No need to get shirty with me. I'm just curious. Not often we have a young single man like that move into town."

Sophie sighed, probably a bit too dramatically. "I'm sorry, I've just got a lot on my mind. I didn't mean to get snappy."

She received a pat on the hand in reply. "I'm being nosy, so I probably deserved it," her mother said, her eyes suddenly gentle, telling Sophie the teasing was over. "But I don't want to hear you say you're not his type." She held up a finger when Sophie went to interrupt. "You're a highly successful surgeon and you're beautiful. I'm sure he'd be more than interested if you were sweet on him."

Sophie decided not to comment. The problem was, she *did* like Lark. He was handsome, kind and engaging. She had no idea whether his flirting was him being a tease or whether he was interested, but the timing was way off for her.

But he was a dad. She had to keep reminding herself of that. And that put him off-limits. The last thing she needed was to spend too much time with his daughter, to expose herself to what she'd never have. What she wanted so badly, when it wasn't ever going to be within her grasp.

Besides, she was only here for a while. She had a career to return to, a house that she needed to move back into in Auckland. In the near future she was going to have to slip back into doctor mode and take up residence at Starship

Children's Hospital again. Go back to the life she'd temporarily run away from.

And deep down, she didn't think Lark would be all that interested in her, not long-term. Aside from the fact that she would be living a two-hour plane ride away, he struck her as the kind of guy who'd put down roots and would want a brood of children running through his house.

And that wasn't in her future.

"You sure you're okay, hon?"

Sophie looked back at her mother and forced a smile. "Yeah, I'm fine. Just a lot to think about."

"Maybe you need to stop helping out so much at the shelter and spend more time relaxing. We could do a few day spas or something."

That sounded good. Better than good. She liked to keep herself busy.

"Sounds like a plan."

"Maybe we should do dinner and a movie tomorrow night, then book a spa for one day next week?"

Hmm. Any night but tomorrow. "I'm actually having dinner with a friend tomorrow night, so we might have to take a rain check on that," she told her. "But yes to the spa."

"Anyone I know?"

"Ah, probably not. You want another coffee?"

Sophie waved the waiter over and ordered two more lattes. The last thing she needed was her mother asking her any more questions about her dinner date tomorrow evening.

She was already tying herself in knots over going. Over being with both Lark and Lucy, like part of their little family.

Argh.

The worst thing was she'd started to really like him, couldn't deny it...until she'd met his daughter.

A part of her hoped he had asked her over because he liked her as more than a friend. And another part of her hoped that something might happen. Even if it was only for fun.

As nice as it was spending time with her mother again and

not having to deal with the pressures of work while she took a sabbatical, spending time with Lark had been like a mini holiday in itself.

Sophie's phone rang.

It was the second time her mobile had saved her today. First from loneliness earlier, now from a further grilling from her mother.

"Hello."

She recognized the voice on the other end straightaway. Her colleague from the shelter, and she could tell something was wrong.

"Sophie, we weren't sure whether to say anything earlier, because you're not used to dealing with this sort of thing like we are, but today we're having to put some of the animals down, the ones that haven't found homes yet. We've got so many more animals coming in, and we can't cope with any more."

Sophie fiddled with her spoon, tapping it in agitation against the cup. Her stomach had started to swirl. She felt sick.

"You're right, I'm queasy just thinking about it."

There was silence for a beat down the other end.

"What I'm phoning to tell you is that we're putting the golden puppy down this afternoon, the one you're always saying you're so fond of. The little ones are usually the first to go to new homes, especially purebreds, but times are hard at the moment and adoptions are down. We can only keep them so long."

Sophie shut her eyes. Oh, God.

She was going to be sick. Actually sick.

She pushed back her chair to stand, looked out at the street full of people.

"I'll take him."

There was silence again. "You need to think this through carefully. We can hold off for a couple days if you're serious and need more time. You don't want to make a decision like this without thinking it through properly."

As if she had a choice. There were things in life she regretted, and looking back and knowing that "thinking it through properly" would mean the end of a beautiful little puppy's life was not something else she needed on her conscience. Sure, he was only one puppy of hundreds that were put down each year across the country, but still. She'd bonded with him from her first day there.

"No, I'll take him. Is it okay if I come past later today? I'll need to get supplies and stuff first."

When she hung up the phone, she wondered what on earth she'd done. But it felt like the right thing.

Now she just had to break the news to her mother that she had another houseguest.

CHAPTER TEN

LARK threw another log on the fire and stood for a moment, watching it hiss and spit. He loved the warmth from a real fire, the way it sent such dry heat through the air and filled a room with a sweet smell that was so hard to describe.

"Whatcha doing, Dad?"

He looked up as his daughter spoke. Lark had thought Lucy was sound asleep in bed. Instead she stood in the doorway, hair mussed up and half out of its ponytail, warm pajamas buttoned up, woolen socks on her feet.

"You should be in bed, miss."

He wasn't so good at telling her off, or insisting she do something, but he was getting better. It was a fine line between being a good father and treading on eggshells in case he upset her. She'd been through a lot, but he had to trust himself and her more.

Lucy was strong, like him.

"I can't sleep."

He walked the few steps back to the sofa and dropped down, picking up the recipe book he'd discarded and patting the spot beside him.

"Come here, rascal."

She scampered over to him, landing on the sofa with a light thud and tucking in under his arm.

Lark dropped a kiss to her head and pulled her close.

"You do realize I should send you straight back to bed, don't you?"

Her answer was to wriggle in tighter, as though she never wanted him to let go.

Lark sighed and pulled the recipe book back onto his lap, leaving his other arm around her. It hurt his back sitting like that, but he wasn't going to moan. He'd suffer all night if it meant his little girl felt safe and loved. And nothing beat having her close like that.

Made him feel loved, too.

He pushed away the thoughts of what he'd left behind. Sometimes he missed it, rodeo-riding for a living, having his name called over the loudspeaker, winning the title belts. The thrill of doing what he loved.

Having a beautiful woman on his arm, proud to be his wife.

He tried not to snarl. Forced his lip not to curl.

Lark hated that Kate had fooled him the way she had. That he'd thought his wife was in love with him, that there was more to their marriage than materialism.

How wrong he'd been.

But he'd never change the past for the world. Would never wish not to have met Kate, or not to have married her.

Because, as bad as the divorce had been, as unsettling as it had been, they'd made a beautiful daughter and he never wanted to let her go. She made everything right, was worth fighting for, and he couldn't imagine a life without her. Not now.

"So what are you doing?" Lucy mumbled again from her spot beside him.

Lark laughed. Just a chuckle, but she sure drew him from his thoughts.

He flicked the book back to the page he'd had it on. A beautiful golden, stuffed turkey was displayed. Surrounded by sides of candied yams, mashed potato and corn on the cob.

Precisely what he'd like to replicate, yet somehow he already knew it was beyond his capabilities.

"I'm trying to teach myself how to cook a turkey."

"Oh." She wriggled forward so she could lean on his knee and look at the book. "Why can't we just buy one all done like that?"

Lark flipped the book shut and ruffled her head. Why hadn't he thought of that? Surely there was someone around who could help him out, somewhere that sold that sort of thing?

Although it wasn't as though anybody else in town would be celebrating the occasion—even Americans wouldn't be cooking their turkeys for another four months at least! Still, it was worth trying…

"Who taught you to be so darn smart, huh?"

Lucy shrugged and looked up at him, her big eyes melting his heart. "You did."

Lark shook his head, wondering how she always seemed to say the right thing.

"To bed, young lady!" he demanded, standing up as she squirreled away. "It's way past lights out."

Lucy shrieked as he chased her.

"To bed!"

By the time he reached her room, pretending to be a monster as she giggled from beneath her blankets, he wondered why he ever even bothered thinking about what he'd once had. Why he wasted the brain power.

He had a beautiful little girl, a new home and horses out in the fields. And he was starting to feel that he was getting the hang of things on his own.

Just because it was only the two of them, it didn't give him a reason to feel sorry for himself. Not ever.

He was luckier than most and it was time he realized it.

"Daddy, can you read me a story?"

Lark fell onto the bed beside her and folded the top blanket back a little. She didn't often ask him to read to her anymore because she had little books of her own she could devour.

But he loved to be asked.

"Just one chapter, okay?"

She fell back against the pillows and sighed. "Okay."

He had a feeling she'd be asleep before he even finished the first page.

Lark arrived home with a bouncing child beside him and a chicken that smelled like heaven on the floor near her feet. Thank goodness he'd managed to get a precooked one!

"Just don't stomp on that bird!"

He doubted Lucy had heard him; she was out the door and racing up the steps to the house the moment the car stopped. Lark retrieved the chicken, plus a few other bags, and headed on in.

The chicken was going to be served at room temperature— it was already cooked to perfection—but he was in charge of the potatoes and some other vegetables, plus heating up the gravy. It didn't sound like too much, but then he wasn't exactly a whiz in the kitchen.

And he needed to have a bit more of a tidy-up. He kept the place as clean as he could, but he wasn't exactly used to having company over.

So long as there were no other distractions aside from racing out to feed the horses, he'd be fine.

And so long as our guest shows up. Something told him that she wasn't entirely comfortable at the prospect of spending the evening here with them.

He hated to admit that he was hoping more than anything else that she would show.

"When's dinner, Daddy?"

Lark groaned.

"It's only four o'clock," he called back. "Dinner's a while off but you can have a snack now."

Lucy wandered into the kitchen as he started unloading the groceries.

"When's she coming?"

Lucy looked thoughtful, climbing up onto the counter to watch him while he sorted through the bags.

"Sophie?"

"Yeah," she said, kicking her heels on the cupboards.

He ignored it. Her mother would have told her off for banging, but so long as she was happy sitting there yapping to him, he wasn't going to be too hard on her. Her being happy was all he cared about.

"I told her to come by after six, I think," he told her.

"And did you ask anyone else for dinner?"

Lark stopped what he was doing and looked at her. He placed his hands one on either side of her and leaned in so they were touching foreheads.

"Lucy Anderson, are you trying to tell me something?"

She giggled, but she didn't move. Instead she pressed her forehead closer so that their noses touched. "No."

"Like that you have a boyfriend you wanted me to ask over?"

"No!" she squealed this time, wriggling so much he grabbed her and held her in place.

"Are you sure?"

He tried not to laugh too hard. They hadn't goofed around like this, joked, in what felt like forever.

Maybe he wasn't doing as badly in the dad stakes as he'd thought.

Lucy rolled her eyes. "I'm too young to have a boyfriend, Dad."

"Well, if you're sure…"

Lucy angled her head and watched him again. More intently. "Does this mean Sophie is *your* girlfriend?"

Oh, heavens, no. He hadn't meant to give her that idea. Not at all.

"No, darlin', Sophie's just a friend. Remember I told you she worked with animals? And that she was helping me with those horses we picked up when it was snowing?"

She seemed content with his answer, jumping down from the counter and landing with a thud.

Lark laughed and refocused on what he was doing. Time

was definitely getting away from him, and at this rate they'd be ordering pizza for dinner. Or eating the chicken on its own.

By the time he turned around Lucy was already gone, her attention diverted elsewhere.

No matter how much he was looking forward to an evening in Sophie's company, he still wasn't convinced that asking her over had been the wise thing to do. Was it tempting fate? And should he even allow himself to be attracted to her when he couldn't offer her anything more than an evening or two of fun? He didn't know if he'd ever want a full-on relationship with a woman again.

Not after the way his marriage had worked out.

Sophie might be a different kind of woman, but it didn't matter. He'd been hurt badly enough to last him a lifetime. Been betrayed one time too many.

Now if he could just get his horses fed, a bottle of decent red wine open and warming in front of the fire and dinner on the table, he'd be able to relax.

Sophie sat in her car outside Lark's house. She liked how familiar she'd become with his place, as though her car could find its way here on autopilot.

Sophie could imagine how beautiful it would be here in spring—foals kicking up their heels as they hurtled around beside their mothers, the fields lush with long green grass.

Part of her, deep inside, longed still to be here when the weather changed and winter made way for a warmer climate. When Queenstown was less of a tourist town once the ski fields had shut for the season and it just felt more like her regular old hometown again.

She sighed. The kind of deep, expressive sigh that would have made anyone around her stop to ask what was wrong.

Sometimes she wondered if she should have just taken what had happened all those years ago as fate. Perhaps falling pregnant then had been a sign that her destiny was to be a mother.

That she was supposed to stay here in Queenstown instead of setting her sights on the biggest city and the biggest hospital.

But there was no point thinking like that. Because she *hadn't* had the baby, and, at the time, coming back home single and pregnant hadn't even seemed like an option.

Keeping her pregnancy and her choices to herself was the one thing she didn't regret. It was knowledge better held inside her, not burdening anyone else. But then, maybe that was her being selfish.

Sophie banished thoughts of her past as she prepared to go inside. It was already dark, but the porch was filled with an eerie series of lights, illuminating the exterior of the home. The curtains were pulled, so she couldn't see in, but when she opened her door she could smell the telltale aroma of smoke in the air—logs and pinecones burning in a roaring fire.

She could picture Lark waiting for her, glass of wine in his hand perhaps, warming his feet in front of the fire.

Sophie found herself smiling.

Maybe tonight had been a great idea after all. If it kept her tucked away from the thoughts that kept haunting her, it had to be good. She needed to compose herself, deal with the fact that he had a little daughter whose company she could also enjoy. That was why she'd chosen her vocation, why she worked in pediatrics—because she loved children. No matter what happened, or what her mistakes had been, no one could ever take that away from her.

She reached for the bottle of wine she'd brought, then thought better of it, grabbing her new puppy instead. He'd just woken up from a deep slumber on the passenger seat, and she put him firmly under her arm.

She could come back for the wine. Without a leash for the pup, which she'd accidentally left behind, she didn't want to risk him running off in the dark. Even if he was a touch too big and heavy to carry.

Sophie lugged him to the door, holding him at an awkward angle so she could knock, and hoping it was okay that she'd brought him. There was noise from inside, a few thumps, then the door swung back.

"Hi!"

Sophie's heart beat hard. This wasn't going to be as easy as she'd talked herself into thinking it would.

Lark's pretty, blonde and blue-eyed girl stood with one hand still on the door handle. She was grinning up at Sophie, lips pulled back in the widest smile Sophie had ever seen, eyes dancing.

Then happiness turned to uberexcitement when she spotted the puppy.

"Oooh! What's his name? Is he for me?"

Sophie managed to catch her breath, to function. "Ah, he doesn't have a name yet. I just picked him up today."

"Did Daddy buy him for me?" Lucy asked, petting the puppy over and over until he became so excited and wriggly that Sophie could barely hold him. "I love him already!" The dog licked frantically at her face.

Sophie's heart plummeted again. She seriously needed to get a grip. She was usually the first person to start chatting with a kid, and now she was all awkward and tongue-tied.

Instead of being her usual confident self, Sophie found that her mouth was as dry as though it was full of cotton wool at the dentist's office.

"May I come in?"

"Dad's in the kitchen," said Lucy, rolling her eyes. "Still."

Sophie wanted to turn and go back to the car, but her arm was almost dead from holding the darn dog, he was so heavy.

"Lucy?" Lark's clear, deep voice rang out down the hall.

Sophie looked up as he appeared, a tea towel slung over his shoulder, watching from the other end of the hall.

"Honey, what's our guest doing standing on the porch in the cold?"

She couldn't take her eyes off him. He was so handsome, so gorgeous in jeans, bare feet and a T-shirt.

Her pulse raced.

But he was a *dad*.

He had a *daughter*.

A daughter she'd fleetingly, the other day, imagined herself caring for. Getting close to.

And that was suddenly harder to deal with than she'd thought.

The desire to run came back, and if it hadn't been for the puppy finally breaking free from her arms and careering off down the hallway, child in pursuit, she would have fled and never looked back.

Lark watched a streak of golden dog race down his hallway followed by his own golden streak of a daughter. He looked back at Sophie, who looked as if she'd seen a ghost. That worried look was all over her face again.

He took the tea towel from his shoulder and walked down to greet her, to bring her in out of the cold and to close the front door behind her. He'd had the fire going for hours now, but the chill from outside was starting to fill the house.

"Happy Thanksgiving!" He tried to sound as jovial as possible, concerned by the still-frozen look on her face.

Lark even stopped to drop a kiss to her cheek in welcome. She remained motionless, turning slowly only when he moved past her to shut the door.

"Ah, bottle of wine. In the car. Sorry, I was going back out to get it."

He walked past her, tried to ignore the fact she wasn't sounding quite as articulate as usual.

"I've got wine ready and waiting, so let's save either of us chancing frostbite by going out in that, shall we?"

She smiled. He hoped he was making progress.

"My only concern is that we have an extra guest for dinner and I've only set the table for three."

He watched as she swallowed. Seemed to be breathing kind of heavily. Didn't laugh at his joke about the dog.

"Today didn't turn out quite as planned," she said.

He raised an eyebrow, taking her arm at the same time to propel her down the hall toward the kitchen.

"I got a puppy."

"So I saw."

"Is it okay that I brought him? I mean, I know it was kind of rude to just let him go like that, but he wriggled and ran off with Lucy."

Lark decided to ignore her shy, almost shell-shocked behavior. Didn't want to fluster her even more than she obviously was. He turned and moved down the hall, pleased that she'd followed him into the kitchen, where, he had to admit, it smelled pretty good.

He looked into the living room and watched as Lucy wriggled around on her back, the puppy licking frantically at her face, alternating between diving toward her head or leaping on top of her chest.

"I think they've made friends."

Sophie took the glass of wine he handed her, held it still as he took his own and let the dark red pinot noir swish delicately around the glass.

"I'm pleased she likes dogs," said Sophie, her voice low. Quieter than usual. "I never thought to ask before I brought him in."

Lark held his glass up to clink against Sophie's, then indulged in a sip.

"Unfortunately, Lucy has a desperate need to add to our family by the purchase of a puppy." He threw Sophie a look over his wineglass. "I'm thinking either you're both in on some kind of a conspiracy—" he poked a thumb toward the two playing "—or this is actually the universe telling me she deserves the Lab she's been asking for."

Lark laughed, surprised that Sophie didn't find it anywhere near as funny as he did. Something was definitely up with her.

"Lark, are you sure you want me here for dinner? I mean for your *family* Thanksgiving dinner?"

Was that all she was worried about?

"I wouldn't have asked you if I wasn't sure," he said softly. "And I have a feeling Lucy likes you. *Especially* now that you've brought a puppy around."

Sophie seemed to relax slightly, but he could still see the tension in her shoulders. She looked beautiful though. Hair waving over her shoulders, a snug sweater hugging her curves, skinny jeans silhouetting her long legs.

She looked *darn* good. Maybe he should have dressed up more himself.

He took another sip of wine then turned back to his cooking. Surprisingly, he hadn't seemed to mess anything up yet, and the less he thought about his attractive guest, the more likely it was to stay that way.

He was almost glad Lucy was here. It meant nothing could happen.

But…he almost wished they were alone, just so he could see what *might* happen…

Sophie was fighting the urge to chug back her wine just to block out the too-happy scene before her. It was like a movie, a happy family movie, and she was watching from the shadows.

She should never have put herself in this position.

Sophie leaned back in her seat, not even trying to drag her eyes away now. Lark was attempting to get his daughter to the table, but she was too busy playing with the puppy. They were both laughing. The puppy was grunting with pleasure, trying to jump up high enough to catch his play-friend, who was now being hefted into the air by her father.

Her sexy, tousled, intoxicating father.

Sophie groaned again and hoped no one heard her.

She did not need to be attracted to a handsome daddy.

Didn't need to be reminded of the happy little family scene she'd never have for herself.

A shiver raced across her skin, leaving the tiny hairs on her arms standing on end. She could feel them, even through her sweater.

"I think she wore the puppy out."

Lark's voice snapped her out of her trance. She looked up to see the puppy stretching, yawning, then tucking his little head down against the carpet to sleep.

Lucy, on the other hand, didn't look tired at all. Her face was flushed from playing, smile fixed, eyes shining.

"Go wash up for dinner," Lark told his daughter, before turning to face Sophie. "I'm going to kill you," he said in a lower voice, at the same time as he topped up her glass. "She just asked me if we could talk you into keeping him for ourselves."

Sophie bit her lip. The puppy would be better off here. Another reminder of how different her life was from Lark's.

"He'd probably like living here with you guys more than being in town with me, to be completely honest."

Lark groaned.

Sophie turned.

Oops. She might have answered a little too loudly. Lucy was standing behind them.

"Does that mean we can have him?" she asked.

Lark nodded at the table, indicating for her to sit down, as he carried in the huge chicken.

"No, it means Sophie was just thinking aloud. Right?"

"Right. I mean…"

The girl was looking her in the eye. Pleading with her, even though she wasn't saying a word.

"It's my birthday soon," Lucy told her, bouncing over to the table. "I asked Dad for a puppy. One just like yours."

Sophie watched as Lucy angled her seat so she could watch her new friend, even though he was still motionless, sleeping.

"He's sooo cute!"

A wave of happiness took her by surprise. She felt wrong being part of their intimate family dinner, but she had to admit the girl was delightful.

If it hadn't been now, in the company of a man she was far too attracted to, after all that had happened over the past few months and with so much playing on her mind, she would have enjoyed Lucy's company. She would have *loved* her company. She liked children and they generally liked her.

Only this time, the child in question—and the father setting the chicken on the table—felt a little too close to home.

As she watched them, the way Lark looked at his daughter and she sat to attention, she decided that they could have the puppy. She'd agreed to take the dog on a whim, to save him, and she was glad she had. But compared to the kind of life he could have here, with a farm to explore, a child to adventure with and someone around all day to hang out with, she'd be selfish to decide anything else.

"I'm not sure how this will taste, but fingers crossed."

"It'll be great, Dad."

Sophie nodded in agreement. "It looks fantastic."

"Dig in. Maybe you could serve the vegetables?"

He stood to carve the bird and Sophie helped herself to potatoes and yams and plenty of other things, trying to ignore the pang she felt at putting smaller portions on Lucy's plate, too. Talk about final nails in the coffin, she thought miserably. Every bit of tonight reminded her of what she'd never do for her own daughter.

She caught Lark's eye as he motioned for her to hold up her plate.

And she wished, wished so hard, that this was real. That she was the wife. The mother.

That this scene was one that was making her happy, instead of making her feel as though her heart had been ripped out and replaced by a weak, limp substitute.

She looked down before he could catch a glimpse of the tears shining in her eyes.

CHAPTER ELEVEN

Lark was still convinced that something was wrong with Sophie, but he wasn't going to make a big deal out of it. There was something there, something that he couldn't quite put his finger on, and she couldn't seem to meet his gaze.

The trouble was, even though she had been quiet since she'd arrived, he liked her. Seriously liked her. Nothing had changed there.

And it was unsettling him. Big-time.

He'd promised himself, had just thought it was a given, that he wasn't going to get involved with another woman again. But it was as if the universe was telling him otherwise, refusing to let him fight the pull he was feeling toward this woman sitting opposite him at the table.

"Please tell me it's good?"

Lucy grinned at him, all elbows as she cut through her food.

"The chicken is brilliant," praised Sophie.

"Turkey," he corrected, throwing her a wink when Lucy wasn't looking. Turkey had been impossible to find, but free-range chicken that *looked* like turkey had been easy.

She smiled back—the sweet, soft smile he'd been waiting for all night. The one she usually gave him, but that had been absent since she'd arrived tonight.

"Turkey," she repeated.

"And now I have to confess that it's the only part of the meal I can't take credit for."

She laughed. It made him smile.

"The deli in town, right?"

He raised both hands. "Guilty as charged."

"Well, you did a great job on everything else."

That made him laugh, pleased to see the happy expression on Lucy's face, too. Her main source of happiness might be stemming from the snoring pup in the other room, but she was happy and that was all that mattered. It was why he'd decided to do this dinner in the first place.

"So, if I'm completely honest, all I did were the vegetables. The, ah, *bird,*" he said, giving Sophie a look, "was from the deli, along with the stuffing and gravy, although I did have to heat that up." When he heard her laugh he kept going, happy that she was loosening up, being more like her usual self, the self he'd gotten to know over the past week or so. "The cranberry sauce was also store-bought, but in the end, I thought if we wanted actually to enjoy eating, that was the best option."

"Mommy used to buy everything, anyway," said Lucy, her attention still on the puppy.

Lark grimaced. "Yeah, she did."

Sophie looked up, seemed to throw him a question mark.

"But Mommy's back in California," he said, feeling he couldn't let that particular question hang over the table for too long. "And maybe she'll come for a holiday one day, huh?"

Lucy beamed at him. "Yeah. Maybe."

"We talked about this the other day, Lark," Sophie said, her voice low. "I told Lucy that I was just like her. It's pretty special having one parent to look after you."

Lark could have jumped up and kissed her. It was exactly what Lucy needed to hear. And he did, too.

Now he knew why they'd both been so relaxed the other day. Lucy must have opened up to Sophie. It made him smile harder than he had in a long while.

He was pleased Sophie didn't think it was too weird—a father with sole custody of his daughter living on the other side of the world to the child's mother. *He'd never have moved her here if he hadn't thought it was the best thing for her.*

A sadness passed over Sophie's face that he couldn't miss. It was the way she looked at Lucy, as though she saw something in his daughter that made her sad. Unhappy.

Lark had a feeling that even if he had hoped something could happen between Sophie and him after Lucy was tucked up in bed, Sophie wasn't feeling quite the same way he was tonight. Something had changed, was bothering her, and he had no idea what it was. It was as if there was a distance between them.

All he knew was that he didn't like it. It was as if she had a guard up, a wall she'd built to keep him at arm's length.

Lucy's wriggling caught his eye.

"May I leave the table now?" she asked.

Sophie wanted to leave. She never should have come in the first place. Everything about tonight was wrong.

She might have been older than Lucy when her own father had left, but she felt a pang of compassion, of deep-set pain for the girl. When her father had walked out, gone off with someone half his age and left her mother with next to nothing, she'd known the pain of a parent's betrayal. And this little girl had a mother who'd given up interest in her.

It made her sick.

But it also made her realize, very clearly, that she shouldn't be here. This child did not need another woman in her life who wasn't going to be around for long, and she wasn't about to become "another woman" to Lark anyway. Maybe, just maybe, she'd have been tempted into a temporary love affair, something fun and casual for a short burst of time, but not now.

Even if she wanted so desperately to be there for Lucy.

Even if, deep down, she wished she could be the child's mother. To care for her and love her as she deserved to be loved by a mother.

"Lucy, why don't you go play with the puppy again?" Lark suggested.

Lucy jumped from her seat as though there was a rocket stowed beneath it, charging back into the adjoining room. Sophie watched as the puppy stretched, sleepy-eyed, until he realized his friend was back to play with him. Then he leaped up, eager as she was, lapping at her face.

"He might need to go outside, since he's just woken up," Sophie said, moving to stand.

Lark reached over and halted her with his touch, the backs of his fingers brushing her arm. It stopped her dead, made her heart hammer, wishing he hadn't connected with her bare skin.

"Lucy, grab the horse rope at the back door and clip it onto his collar. You can take him outside for his toilet stop."

"Are you sure?" Sophie asked. It might have been her chance to slip away early. She *needed* to get away. Needed an excuse.

Lark's hand fell away from her forearm, but not before his eyes met hers. Something unsaid passed between them, something Sophie didn't want to acknowledge.

She remembered that look. Knew it only too well from the other day in his truck. When he'd watched her, looked at her, leaned in and almost kissed her.

She'd known it had meant something then, and now there was no doubt left in her mind that she hadn't been imagining it. Only now she wasn't sure if she wanted it. Or whether she *should* want it.

Sophie bit the inside of her mouth as a shudder trawled its way with slow intensity down her back, tingling across her shoulders.

When every bone, muscle and fiber in her body screamed at her to want him, to let herself say yes to anything that might, that could happen, why did her mind tell her *no* so firmly? With such determination?

She knew why; she wasn't ready for this. Didn't want to be exposed to Lark's family life, not when she could never grasp it in the future for herself.

But still, his eyes held hers, captured hers. She was like a hopeless fish caught in an expert fisherman's net.

She only hoped she'd be better able to escape.

"Sophie, you seem kind of quiet tonight," he said, once the child and dog had disappeared.

His words were kind, softly spoken. Genuine concern shone from his eyes.

"I'm fine," she assured him, knowing full well she was far from fine. "I'm, well, tired I guess."

He nodded, a thoughtful expression on his face.

"If you say so."

That got her back up. Bristles and all. "What do you mean by that?"

He shrugged, clearly unconcerned by her tone. "You don't seem like your usual self, that's all. Looks to me like something's troubling you, and all I wanted was to make sure that that something wasn't me."

Sophie looked down at her plate, then fiddled with the napkin resting over her knees. "It's not you, Lark. Honestly it's not. I've just got a lot going on right now."

He smiled, but this time it was different, as if he understood.

She relaxed. He wasn't going to pry, she could sense it.

"I know what that's like, believe me."

Since he had an ex back in the States and a daughter to care for, she didn't doubt him.

"Can we just leave it at that?" she asked.

He nodded. "Sure can. But not before I thank you for the other day. Whatever you said to her must have helped."

They watched one another for a moment before he stood up. She didn't know what to say.

"How about another glass of wine, since neither of us want to talk about our problems?"

Sophie shook her head. "I really shouldn't, not when I have to drive back into town."

He placed both hands on the back of his chair and leaned

forward. "You could always stay over, if you don't want to drive."

She couldn't help the burning heat that hit her cheeks at his words. Embarrassed from the intense way he watched her, eyes skimming hers, laughter dancing in their dark depths.

"Sorry—teasing," he said, raising both hands in mock surrender. "But you've only had a small glass. I'm sure you could have a tiny bit more."

Sophie nodded, holding her glass out and trying to regain her confidence. "Just a little more, then," she choked out.

She really had to leave.

And soon.

She stood up to help clear the table while he went back to the kitchen to fill their wineglasses. She was nervous, her hands shaking, enough for her to see them tremble.

She walked the plates into the kitchen, stopping only when she saw Lark watching her. He held both wineglasses, each half-full, and he was leaning back against the counter.

His dark, chocolate eyes were somehow smiling at her, teasing her, making her belly flip hard, over and over again.

Sophie looked down, moved past him, put the plates down. She suddenly felt claustrophobic, didn't know where to look, what to do, where to go.

"Sophie." He said her name in that casual drawl of his, as though the word itself was laced with sweetness.

Her legs turned to liquid.

Make that, dripping in buttery sweetness.

She turned half her body, too scared to face him front-on.

She watched as he put both glasses down and slowly crossed the space between them. Sophie tried not to hold her breath, but she couldn't do anything else.

"There's something I've been wanting to do," he said, his tone low. Soft yet strong.

Sophie watched him. She couldn't do anything *but* watch him.

He leaned toward her. She knew she should move away,

should take the step backward that told him she needed space between them. That she didn't want whatever it was that he'd been wanting to do. Because it was wrong.

But she couldn't.

Not after so many days of thinking about him. Of seeing him. Of *wanting* him.

Lark raised his hand to her chin, two fingers curling gently against her skin, cupping her face to tilt her head back. She didn't even try to resist. Couldn't.

He shuffled closer, just his body, so close to her that she could feel the heat from him.

"Sophie," he said, before dipping his head low, crushing his lips to hers with such tenderness that she barely felt the touch at all.

Hardly felt the pressure of it, but felt the warmth of him everywhere. She sighed into his mouth, wanting so hard to pull away and yet desperate to melt against him, press her body into his and never let go.

Lark's hand moved from her chin to touch her cheek, the softest press of his palm against her, his lips moving more firmly against hers.

Then it was over.

He pulled away so abruptly she was left openmouthed and breathless. Empty. Alone. Standing in his kitchen, wondering what had happened and where that had even come from.

"Lucy's back inside," he said, voice gruff.

Sophie raised a hand to her mouth, touched her lips.

Then looked up at Lark. His eyes were soft, tender, the look on his face so gentle that it had the potential to make her heart melt.

And then Lucy appeared, all red-faced and happy-looking.

Thank goodness he'd heard her come in and she hadn't walked in on them.

"He's been to the toilet," his daughter announced proudly.

Sophie nodded. Lark put his arm around his daughter's

shoulders and squeezed. "Good work. Maybe you *are* almost ready for a puppy, huh?"

Lucy let out a delighted squeal.

It was too much for Sophie.

The kiss, Lark, his daughter…just being here was more than she could cope with. She should have left before it got to this point. Before it became too much.

"Thanks for a lovely dinner," she said, hoping her voice sounded stronger than it felt. "It's been great but I really have to go."

Lark looked at her, confusion on his face, eyebrows knotted. Lucy only looked, not saying anything.

"Are you sure? We haven't even had dessert yet."

She ignored the hurt she sensed in his voice. The confusion.

But she had to go. Had no other option but to leave. Right now.

"It's only ice cream, but…"

"I'm sorry," she said, before scooping up the puppy and trying her hardest to smile at Lucy.

"Will you bring him back to play?"

"Sure," she answered, prepared to say anything so long as it meant she could escape. "Thanks for entertaining him tonight."

"Sam," Lucy called out as Sophie headed toward the door.

She stopped, looked back, watched as Lark left his daughter's side to follow her.

"I'd call him Sam," Lucy said.

Sophie continued toward the door.

When she got there, Lark stopped her, walking in front of her so his frame filled the doorway.

"What's happening here?" he asked, his face worried, drawn.

She refused to look at him.

"I'm sorry, Lark, truly I am."

Then she pushed past him and walked out, sucking in deep

gulps of freezing-cold air as she hurried to her car. She dumped the puppy in the passenger seat and moved around to the other herself.

She wanted to, but she never looked back.

She just drove away as tears filled her eyes, burning the back of her throat, and she fought not to let them fall. Didn't allow herself to give in to them.

He was just a man.

With a daughter. With a *Lucy*.

He didn't mean anything to her, and that's why she had to walk away. Before she got sucked into something that she *couldn't* walk away from.

Before she experienced more of what she could never have herself.

Before she started to yearn for his daughter, too. Because even though she'd tried so hard to keep her distance, she'd fallen for his little girl, as well.

Sophie sobbed then, one big gulp of tears.

She reached for the puppy, one hand steady on the wheel, the other caressing his fur.

Then she fought the emotion in her throat again, refusing to acknowledge it—let alone let it out.

CHAPTER TWELVE

THREE days later, Lark was steaming. Furious. The more he thought about Sophie, the wilder he became with himself.

He'd thought she was different and yet she'd run out on him. Just like his wife had.

He'd pledged to himself to remain single, and what had he done the moment a pretty, charming woman had crossed his path? Almost become involved, that's what.

Lark smiled as a very happy Lucy walked past on her new pony, Cleo.

"Best present in the world?" he asked.

She grinned. "Best ever."

The pair had bonded immediately, from the moment he'd taken her out to the field, blindfolded, to meet her horse. And now she was already having her second ride of the day. Thank goodness the pony was obliging.

"I love her," Lucy told him as she circled past. "She's the best."

He laughed, almost forgetting his woman troubles. "I can see that."

She seemed to have forgotten about the puppy today, for now anyway, although she'd talked about Sam nonstop since Sophie had visited that night.

The night she'd walked out on them and not been in touch since.

"Can I go faster?"

He watched as Lucy came past again. "Sure, ask her to trot. Squeeze your legs lightly and sit up nice and tall."

"I do know how to ride, Dad," she told him, although she was still grinning.

Lark laughed at her; he couldn't do anything else. He probably wouldn't have listened to his own father either, had he been trying to tell him what to do, and she was naturally gifted. She did know what she was doing.

"Come on, then, show me how it's done."

And she did, expertly moving into a trot and riding Cleo out in a big circle.

It was what he needed, to watch her having fun like that. Took his mind off the woman who was still managing to cause him an itch beneath his skin.

She'd been no better than his ex. He'd made a bad judgment call. And he certainly shouldn't have ever introduced her to Lucy or brought her into his home.

Maybe he was a bad judge of character when it came to women. Maybe it was a wake-up call telling him to remain single.

Either way, whatever the case, he needed to forget about her and focus on his role as a father to Lucy. That was all that mattered and he'd temporarily lost sight of the fact that he didn't need a woman in his life.

He didn't need Sophie and he wasn't going to spend any more time thinking about her. Or how she'd walked out.

Even if stopping his mind from thinking about her was like trying to keep a fish alive out of water.

Sophie was taking time out from her time-out. She'd called in sick again to the animal shelter. Not that she had to—her role was purely voluntary and they seemed surprised every time she turned up, they had so few volunteers. But after what had happened the other night...

She still shuddered thinking about how it had ended.

The puppy curled up beside her, tighter, snuggled on the sofa and into her blanket. It was silly, but every time she pressed her face or hand into his fur, she thought of little Lucy. Of her smiling face, of the way she'd so genuinely loved the puppy from the moment she'd set eyes upon him.

And wanted to call him Sam, she reminded herself.

Or the way the girl's father had looked as she'd fled from his house so rudely.

She closed her eyes again, trying to block out the image of his hurt-filled expression, the confusion on his face—followed by what she was sure was a flash of anger.

She couldn't blame him though. He'd put so much effort into the evening, preparing a lovely meal and then…

Another thing she didn't want to think about.

The kiss.

The spine-numbing, lip-tingling kiss that she hadn't been able to forget no matter how hard she tried.

The way his mouth had felt against hers, the look in his eyes before he'd bent and closed the distance between them. And the kindness, the gentleness of his face as he'd pulled away.

Sophie sighed.

She didn't know what he'd wanted from her, what he might have expected. And maybe he didn't, either. But she wasn't ready for whatever might have transpired.

She was here to spend some time on her own, find herself again and deal with her past. With the nightmares that continued to plague her. With the realities she had to face before moving on and taking up her position as a surgeon again. Before slotting into her old life.

There was no way she was ready for a relationship.

And what if something deeper had developed between her and Lark? What then?

She'd have to complicate things by admitting to Lark that she couldn't ever have children. That he'd never have any more kids to add to his brood. Never be able to give Lucy a brother or sister in the future if they stayed together.

And something within her, something she couldn't ignore,

knew that Lark had introduced her to his daughter for a reason. He'd wanted her to know, to show her his life, and she couldn't deal with it. She wasn't ready for confronting that kind of situation.

She owed Lark an apology, but for now she was going to avoid him.

No one liked an ostrich with its head buried in the sand, but it was what she had to do right now.

Tomorrow she was going to pick herself up, shake herself off and deal with life again.

There was a local horse show on and she could go and watch that. Eat hot dogs and chips, guzzle some fizzy drinks, pretend that she had nothing better in the world to be doing. The more junk food the better, just for one day.

Then she was going to suck up the courage to apologize to Lark.

She snuggled back into the sofa, eyes shut, smiling as her puppy snored away beside her, oblivious to her troubles.

He was the only family she had on her radar now, as good as it was going to get for her, so she'd better get used to it and enjoy him.

No wallowing over happy families. Or men she wouldn't appeal to. Or what she couldn't have.

She had a better life than many, and it was time she dealt with it and moved on.

Sophie stood on the sidelines, picking at a plate of hot fries, and watched the horses circling. She loved watching them jump, especially the ponies with their pint-size riders.

One came past her now, a pretty pinto pony with black-and-white markings. Its rider had a braid flying out behind her, but no number on her back. Sophie guessed she must be here to practice, not compete.

She stepped back, smiling as the little rider went past. And then...

Her smile turned to a gasp as a large horse came careering

past, too fast, clipping the tiny pony on the side as they thundered out of control.

The pony tried its hardest, but it stumbled sideways, sending its rider tumbling.

Ouch.

Sophie moved fast, dropping her fries, running to the rider's assistance. The girl had fallen hard, the pony treading on her as it tripped before righting itself.

She was there within an instant, at the girl's side.

"It's okay, sweetheart, I'm a doctor," she said, placing a hand on the girl's chest to keep her lying down flat. "You're going to be just fine."

The child looked up at her. And it was only then that Sophie recognized the blue eyes, now fast filling with tears.

"Lucy?" she asked.

The little head nodded. Sophie's heart started beating that bit too fast.

The stakes had just been raised.

Any child was important, but this one was Lark's precious daughter.

"I'm going to check your head first, make sure you haven't hurt your neck or back, then I'll move you."

"I want my daddy," she whimpered.

"I'm here."

Sophie didn't look up, kept her focus on Lucy, even as the deep, strong voice belonging to Lark joined her.

Lark knelt beside her, one hand on his daughter's chest, as if to calm her, the other holding her hand.

"Where's Cleo?" Lucy cried.

He bent over and pressed a kiss to her hand. "She's fine. Someone's looking after her."

"She didn't mean it, Dad. It wasn't her fault."

Sophie looked up then, met his gaze. She'd seen what happened herself, and Lucy was right. The pony *had* tried her hardest.

"Would you mind telling me what you're doing?" Lark's

question was said in a low voice, but there was no denying the fury in his gaze.

She recoiled, scared of being so close to him. But she had a job to do, and she wasn't going to let her feelings for Lark affect her assessment of the situation.

Lucy had taken a bad tumble.

"Sophie?" he questioned her again.

"I'm a doctor, Lark. She's in good hands."

If Lark was surprised he didn't say anything.

At least he seemed to believe her.

Sophie gently eased off Lucy's helmet, felt her over carefully, then moved on to her arms. She knew straightaway that one was broken.

"Aaarghh," Lucy moaned. "It hurts so bad."

Sophie looked up at Lark, focused now, no longer worried about any looks he may or may not be giving her.

"We need to get her to the hospital. This arm is broken, and I want her X-rayed straightaway."

"Can I lift her?"

Sophie locked eyes with him. Saw that right now he didn't care what had passed between them. All he cared about was his little girl and making sure she was okay.

"You lift her, carefully, and I'll support her arm," she instructed. "I'd prefer to ice it, or not move her at all, but we don't have a choice."

He lifted his daughter so gently it was as though he was lifting a broken, shattered doll and trying not to lose even the tiniest of pieces.

"I've got an ice pack in a cooler in the truck," he said, before dropping a kiss to his daughter's head, his lips touching her hair. "I always have one on hand for the horses."

Sophie nodded, but before Lark could even see her movement Lucy was sobbing again.

"Honey, where does it hurt? Tell me."

Lark's voice was desperate, a crack in his throat.

"I don't want to leave without Cleo," she cried. "Put her in the truck, *please*."

Lark looked at Sophie. She looked back at him.

"Taking a few minutes to get her pony isn't going to matter," she assured him, siding with Lucy if only because of the look on her face. "Let's get her back to the truck, you grab Cleo, then we can go."

Lark didn't look happy about the situation, but he didn't argue. She doubted he ever would when it came to his daughter.

They'd been at the hospital for more than three hours. Lark was exhausted, drained from the worry, and now he was starting to panic over the snow that had begun to fall outside. He was most worried about his daughter, but he had to get Cleo out of the truck and get home to check the other horses, too.

If he didn't go soon, he was concerned the road might be too dangerous to navigate. Especially once it was dark. But at the same time he wasn't going to leave his girl.

Lark walked back down the corridor, tasteless cup of coffee in his hand, and almost ran smack-bang into Sophie.

"Hey," she said.

He held up a spare coffee he'd poured. "Didn't know how you like it, but I went with white and one sugar."

She took the cup from him and blew on the hot liquid.

"She doing okay?" he asked.

Sophie sipped then reached out a hand to touch him. Her hand trailing down his arm, squeezing, then letting go.

He wished he didn't like it so much, but he did. He was still annoyed with her, but mostly he was grateful she'd been on hand to help. Even if he was confused.

She sure had a lot of explaining to do.

"Lucy fell asleep the moment you walked out the door," said Sophie, turning back to the room she'd come from so he could look in the tiny window.

"She looks so small, lying there like that," he said. "So—I don't know, vulnerable."

The pink cast covering his daughter's lower arm made him cringe.

Lark swallowed another sip of coffee to get rid of the lump of emotion straining to be released. He cleared his throat.

"You know, it wasn't the pony's fault," Sophie said to him. "I saw the whole thing happen. The other rider was an adult and she really should be held accountable."

"I shouldn't have let her ride there," he said, still seeing his little girl lying on the ground, worrying that she'd done herself a serious injury. "She was so desperate to take the pony down there, to ride her, and I couldn't say no to her. Can't ever seem to say no."

"I'm not going to tell you to stop beating yourself up over this, because I know you can't not be a father," Sophie said to him, taking a step back. "But she's going to be fine, and I think the best thing you can do is follow the doctor's orders, leave her here until morning and then take her home."

That was the last thing Lark wanted to do. He'd rather sleep by her side and not let her spend a moment alone.

But he did have to get back home. Maybe he could go to the farm, do what he had to do, then be at the hospital before she woke up again...

"There will be a nurse assigned to her. Because of her age she won't be left alone once she's awake. They'll call you straightaway if anything changes."

He still wasn't sure.

"I don't want her to think I've abandoned her," he admitted, feeling that chunk of emotion rise up in his throat again.

Sophie didn't say anything, she just looked at him.

And something told him that part of her, whatever it might be, understood what he was trying to say.

"She knows you love her," Sophie told him, her head down, voice so soft he could hardly hear her. "Lucy knows she's the most important thing in your life. She's not going to think you've left her."

Lark knew Sophie was right. Deep down he knew, but walking away from his daughter was still hard.

"And she'll probably sleep until morning anyway. They gave her pain relief and it's best if she's under observation for the night. It was a decent fall."

"I know," he said, looking through the window one last time. "I know it was."

He walked past Sophie to go in to Lucy. If he was going to leave her, he wanted at least to kiss her goodbye first.

Before he opened the door, he turned back to Sophie.

"I really appreciate what you did today."

She shook her head, one arm wrapped around her body, the other still holding her now-empty cup.

"It's what I do."

He frowned. He couldn't help it. "Yeah, about that," he said, staring at her, hard. "I think you have some explaining to do."

She looked embarrassed, but she didn't look away, maintained eye contact with him. This was a different Sophie to the one he was used to. This woman wasn't as shy, she was more confident. There was something more courageous, stronger, about her.

"I'm a doctor, Lark. I'm taking some time off, but that's what I do for a living."

He sighed. "You doing anything tonight?"

She looked wary. "Why?"

"Because I'm about to go out into the snow and head for home, and since you don't have a car here I think you should come with me and explain on the way."

She gulped. He saw the movement.

"Okay?" he asked.

She flushed slightly, the confident doctor starting to disappear.

"Okay," she muttered.

He didn't give her a chance to change her mind. Instead he

walked into Lucy's room and hoped Sophie hadn't bolted the moment he turned away.

His back ached, more than ever, as it always did when he was stressed or tired. But he ignored it.

He had more important things to think about than his back. Or the fall. Or dealing with this alone.

All that mattered was Lucy.

CHAPTER THIRTEEN

SOPHIE was nervous. She didn't want to spend any more time with Lark, but she hadn't had the heart to turn him down. Not when he was clearly so upset, so devastated about what had happened to Lucy.

And she did have some explaining to do. Maybe she didn't necessarily owe it to him, but he'd been nothing but kind to her, and she hadn't exactly been truthful.

She watched him through the window, almost turned away because she felt as if she was intruding somehow on a private moment between father and daughter. But she couldn't *not* look. Her eyes drank their fill of the handsome man bent over his child, lips whispering across her forehead, hand caressing her hand, before he turned away.

He saw her, his eyes locked on hers as he stood to walk from the room.

"I don't feel right leaving her," he said, voice gruff.

"I know."

She doubted she did know. Couldn't really know, since she wasn't a parent, but the anguish on his face said it all.

"Let's go," he said, looking into the room one last time before pulling on his jacket and turning away.

Sophie followed him, staying a distance away, careful not to walk too close. Not to brush against him. After seeing him again, all she knew was that she had feelings for him that she had no choice but to ignore.

"Will the pony be okay?"

Lark kept walking, but slowed his pace slightly. "Yeah, she'll be fine. Tired, but fine."

They didn't say anything else until Lark pushed open the double doors at the exit to the hospital.

"Jeez, it's freezing out here!"

He grabbed hold of her hand, tucking it against his and pulling her toward the truck. "Don't slip."

Snow fell lightly down on her head, skimming her nose, touching her cheeks. She had a sweater and jeans on, not enough to keep her warm, but they were moving fast.

She tried to ignore Lark's palm against hers, the strength of his hold, but it wasn't easy. He never looked at her, only took her to the truck, unlocking her door before making his way around to the driver's side.

She jumped in; he landed beside her. It wasn't like the other day in his truck, when they'd been so close, but it was still intimate. There was still the sense that they were breathing the same air, that they were alone together, that...

"So you're a doctor."

He said it as a statement. His voice was flat.

Sophie wriggled a little away from him, all too aware of what she had to tell him. What she had to admit. Her whole life story.

"I'm only here on holiday," she said, looking out the window into the darkness to avoid Lark. "Kind of an extended sabbatical from my job." She laughed, a low noise in her throat that escaped before she could stop it. "Actually a sabbatical from my life, if I'm really honest."

Lark didn't say anything for a while. She was pleased. The snow was still falling, heavier now, and he had the wipers on fast as he peered out the window intently.

"Going back to the part where you're a doctor..." he said, a hint of sarcasm in his voice.

She sighed.

May as well just get it all out there on the table.

"I'm actually a surgeon," she said, glancing at him this time. Wanting to see his reaction.

"A surgeon," he repeated, his voice giving none of his feelings away.

His expression didn't change; he was still focused on the road. She was pleased they weren't sitting facing one another. At least she didn't have to look into his eyes as she spoke. She could avoid seeing what he thought of what she was saying.

"I live in Auckland mostly, about two hours away by plane," she told him. "Usually my life consists of working as a pediatric surgeon at Starship Children's Hospital. I spend my day wearing a white coat, talking to parents and other doctors about treatment options, and trying to save little people from all sorts of problems."

"I see."

If he was particularly shocked he didn't show it.

"I should have told you, but I'm taking some time off from that life right now. I didn't want to be that person while I was here."

He briefly glanced at her, but his eyes quickly refocused on the road.

"You don't have to explain."

But she did. He wanted to know and she felt she had to tell him.

"I didn't mean to lie to you, Lark," she told him truthfully. "I just needed to escape that life while I was back here. I wanted to be a different person for a while, so I could think and reflect about what I'd run away from. There are things I couldn't deal with, and it was time for me to take a break."

He stayed silent.

"I'm helping out at the animal shelter on a volunteer basis, and I don't have to be back at my real job for a few more months."

"So you're hiding out here and running away from something," he said.

"I wouldn't say running away exactly."

"I'm not judging you, Sophie. I've run away from my own problems too, so you're not exactly alone there," Lark told her.

"Maybe you're right. Maybe I am running," she admitted, "but I don't want to run. I want to figure things out, and it seemed like a good idea at the time to come back here. To come home."

He laughed, a small chuckle that caught her by surprise.

"You've run *back* home and I've run away from home," he told her. "We might have different reasons, but in the end we've both hidden from our problems."

She leaned back in the seat, actually pleased she'd opened up to him, told him what she'd done and why she was here. Or at least part of it.

"Maybe we haven't hidden from our problems, Lark. Maybe we were simply smart enough to offer ourselves a fresh start." She paused. "You've left something behind that clearly wasn't working for you, and you've started over."

"I still ran," he said, "but I'm pleased I did. It was the right thing for me, for Lucy, too. But you? I have a feeling you're not so sure about your decision."

Sophie looked out the window again, hardly able to see anything. The ground was covered in white and the snow was still falling.

"I should have stayed and dealt with my problems, but instead I came back here, thinking, somehow, that it would make everything right. That I'd have some time out and be ready to go back to how things were," she told him.

She recognized the motion as the truck pulled into Lark's driveway, the start of the incline.

In a way she was relieved they were back at his place, but then that also meant she was going to be alone with him. In his house. Without his daughter as an excuse.

The home ahead looked dark, there were no lights on. His roof was covered in white; it was all she could really make out.

"How about I give you the keys so you can head in and open

up? I'll drive around the side, take Cleo off and feed the other horses."

She nodded her agreement, holding out her palm for the keys as he idled outside the house.

"There's firewood in the basket if you want to light the fire, get the house warm, and help yourself to anything you need. A sweater, just whatever," he said, his voice slightly gruff. "You know, because you look a little cold."

Sophie took the keys, hopped out of the truck and walked in the light made by his headlights. She carefully trod up the steps to the door, turned the key and let herself in, fumbling for the light switch.

It was cold in the house, but not as cold as it was outside.

Sophie stood in the hallway, the door shut behind her, as the truck lights disappeared and dipped around to the side of the house.

She couldn't help but think about the last time she'd been here. How nice the night could have been, but how badly it had ended because of her.

Now she was alone in his home, about to start a fire and boil some water for a coffee. To look through his fridge and try to find something that she could make into dinner, since neither of them had eaten since goodness only knew when.

In a way it seemed too intimate, being in his house like this. Although something about it also seemed…special.

She wasn't sure which was worse, but right now she needed to get the house warm. Pull the curtains and try to remember how to start a fire, rather than just push a button for a gas one to ignite.

Sophie walked through to the living room first and closed the curtains in there, but not before she peeked outside again. The snow had started to fall fast and heavy, and she had a feeling it was only going to get worse. They often had snow here, but this was worse than usual. Especially this early in the season.

She hoped Lark had a radio so they could tune in and see

what the local weather report was, because something told
her the roads were probably close to being shut now, if they
weren't already.

She gulped.

Which would mean she could be stuck here, alone, with
Lark all night.

Until morning.

Lark made his way slowly across the yard to the house. He
would usually go in the back door, but he'd locked it and he
doubted Sophie would hear him if he knocked.

The weather had taken a turn for the worse. The only conso-
lation was that it was still snowing, so the air felt almost still.
It was when the wind picked up and the rain started pelting
down with fury that it was terrible.

He pulled off his boots at the front door and let himself in.
Strangely, it didn't feel like his home tonight. He could hear
the television going, not loud but enough of a hum for him
to detect. There were lights on throughout the house, and he
could smell something cooking.

It was like arriving home to the kind of domestic scene he'd
always expected he'd have. His wife had been beautiful, and
they'd had plenty of seemingly good years together before everything had started to unravel, but arriving home had never
felt like this.

The only thing missing was Lucy, but he didn't want to
think too much about her. It would only send him hightail-
ing it back to the hospital, and the last thing either of them
needed was him driving in this weather. Besides, they'd told
him rather forcefully to stay away.

He walked into the kitchen.

And stopped.

Sophie had let her hair down to fall around her shoulders,
and her head was bent. She was busy chopping something on
the counter.

He was still angry with her. Even though she'd helped him with Lucy today.

He was still annoyed at how she'd left the other night. Out of sorts about the fact that he'd thought he'd connected with her, that there was something between them, and he hadn't known about her, not truly, at all.

But seeing her like this, in his kitchen?

Lark gulped.

She was something else.

He listened to her hum as she kept her hands busy, turning to the stove then back to the counter again.

And then she looked up.

Light brown—hazel—eyes met his, her expression widening as she realized he was standing there.

"Lark! You gave me a fright."

He crossed the room. "Sorry, I was just admiring the view."

She blushed. Bright, tomato-sauce red.

"I mean..." he stammered. That had come out all wrong. "Well, you look great, but I meant I was admiring seeing someone else in my kitchen. Arriving inside to find a meal under way and the house warm isn't something I'm used to anymore."

He watched as her shoulders visibly relaxed.

"It's only an omelet, and I'm not convinced the fire is going that well," she told him.

Lark went over to check it. "Doesn't look bad to me, and it's still a heap warmer in here than it is outside."

He opened the door on the large fireplace and threw in another log before poking the fire vigorously then closing the door.

"I didn't know if you had a radio, but I managed to catch the end of the news on the television when I first came in," she said, standing over a pan filled with an almost-golden omelet.

"Roads closed?"

She grimaced. "Yeah. They're saying it's the worst storm in the area for almost twenty years."

"Typical."

She turned to look over her shoulder at him. Lark had to resist walking up behind her and placing his hands there, covering her shoulders and upper arms. Connecting with her.

"What's typical?" she asked.

"That when I decide to move here the weather packs in."

Sophie reached for the plate she had beside the stove and expertly flipped the omelet onto it.

"You've got to admit that it's pretty beautiful though," she said, followed by a sigh. "If you're tucked up inside with a fire, a glass of wine and good company, then it's not half-bad."

He walked toward her, unburdening her of the plate.

Was she referring to him as good company or just making a statement in general?

"Is this mine?"

Sophie glanced at him, eyes partially hidden by her lashes.

God, she was beautiful.

All the anger, annoyance, he'd felt toward her earlier simply disappeared over one look. One connection.

What he'd felt for her before she ran out on him the other night had been real. No matter how much he didn't want to become involved or told himself she wasn't for him.

There was something between them and they both knew it.

"I, ah, didn't know what you'd want in yours, so I just worked with what I could find."

They were still looking at one another, but Sophie kept glancing away. He couldn't have cared less what was in the omelet. What he liked was the fact that she'd made it for him, and that she was standing in front of him right now.

"I'll like it," he said.

"There's tomatoes, onions, cheese…"

Lark put the plate down on the counter. He didn't take his eyes off her.

She looked frightened, as though she didn't know what to do, but she didn't move away.

He leaned past her, turned off the gas on the stove and then stood before her, arms hanging at his sides.

"I don't care what's in the damn omelet, Sophie."

She tilted her face back up toward him.

"You don't?"

He shook his head, the smallest movement from side to side.

"All I care about is why you walked out on me the other night. Why you ran like that."

There. He'd said it. Gotten it off his chest.

He needed to know, damn it!

"I don't know what to say to you," she said.

Lark could see she was being honest. He doubted, now that he was standing before her and looking into her eyes, that she'd easily lie or deceive anyone.

His ex-wife had started to make him think that all women behaved a certain way, but what he could see in Sophie's eyes told him that maybe he'd been right about her from the start.

"Tell me the truth, Sophie," he told her. "I need to know why you walked out."

She looked as though she was going to cry.

Lark had the overwhelming urge to open his arms to her, to fold her against him and hold her. He felt that was what she needed, but he wasn't sure *what* to do. Whether that was the right thing, what it would mean to her if he did it.

"Sometimes it's the truth that hurts the most," she said, her voice low.

Her face was tilted down, shoulders slumped slightly, but he wasn't having it. He did reach for her then, knew it was the right thing to do, drew her into his arms.

She hesitated for a beat, seemed unsure, before taking the final step toward him, falling against him. Tenderly at first, and then deeper into his embrace as he folded his arms around her.

Lark had thought he'd feel uncomfortable, holding her like that, but it seemed the most natural thing in the world. He let his lips fall to the top of her head, not kissing her but allowing them to sit there, inhaling the smell of her. Enjoying the feel of her slim, womanly body in his arms. Touching him, length to length.

He didn't want to ask, but he felt he had to. Needed to know, even if the answer wasn't the one he hoped it would be.

"Was it because of Lucy? The reason you walked out?" he said, the words low, lips hardly raised from her head.

Lark was holding his breath. He wanted the answer to be no, wished it to be.

She didn't say anything, only nodded.

His body stiffened, even though he tried hard to stop it from doing so. She hadn't said why, there was still so much left unsaid, but Lucy was his everything. He could compromise, he wasn't set in his ways, but Lucy was the one thing he'd never change. He would never compromise her happiness for the sake of anything. Maybe it was because she'd gone through something similar to his daughter. Or maybe it was something else.

Sophie didn't look up at him and didn't say anything else. She turned back to the stove, flicked the gas and stirred her egg mixture to pour into the pan.

Lark didn't know what to do, what to say, all over again. So he collected his plate and moved to sit at the table.

He could see she needed a moment to compose herself, and he was starving hungry. Maybe eating something would help him deal with whatever it was she was about to say.

It had been a long day, he was tired and he didn't want to say anything he would regret later. Not when she hadn't had a chance to explain herself.

He focused on his food, then changed his mind, unable to ignore the beautiful woman in his kitchen. While he ate he watched her, the way she moved, body elegant and fluid. Then she placed her own omelet on a plate and faced him again.

She was clearly unsure of what to do.

"Come and join me."

Sophie looked hesitant but she did as he'd suggested. She

walked slowly, put her plate down on the table and sat across from him.

"I hope you're good at board games," he said, trying to kill the tense atmosphere.

Sophie finished her mouthful then smiled, hesitantly. "You think we'll be stuck for a while?"

"Yeah, I'd say."

She went back to her food, eating each mouthful slowly, as though she didn't want to have to sit and talk, happy to do something to avoid chatting.

Just as he was about to get up, to go and look out the window or try to tune in the radio, Sophie put her knife and fork down.

She sighed. A deep, belly-filled exhale of breath that made him stop, compelled him to sit back in his seat.

"Lark, it's not because I don't like Lucy," she told him. "She's a gorgeous child and you should be proud of her. I had a great time with her the other day."

"But?" he asked, eyes trained on her.

"Why does there always have to be a *but,* right?"

Yeah. His life sometimes felt as if it had been changed by a series of *buts.*

"You've got your reasons, Sophie. You don't have to tell me."

She looked almost tearful. Clearly it was hard talking about whatever it was that was troubling her.

"I work with children every day," she explained. "Well, back in my usual life."

He nodded, happy to listen so long as she was comfortable talking.

"Before I decided to take a break, I had a hard time. I'm used to losing patients, it's part and parcel of the job, but a little girl I'd known for years as she came in and out of hospital, well, she died on my table."

Lark could see the genuine pain in her eyes, wished he didn't have to see how much talking about this hurt her. But at the same time he wanted to hear. Wanted to know her back-ground, what troubled her, so he could understand her.

"Telling her parents, when they loved her so much and had fought for her for so long, was dreadful. I've done it so many times before, had to be the bearer of bad news, but this one hit me hard." She paused. "She was the same age as your Lucy."

Lark waited.

"She was four years old when I first met her as a perky little kid, and the last time I saw her she was a cancer-ridden seven-year-old."

"I'm so sorry, Sophie."

He should never have been so hard on her. So judgmental.

"Her name was Rose and I don't think I'll ever forget her."

Lark didn't know what to do, other than look away to give Sophie the privacy to brush away her tears.

He swallowed. Thought of how his own little girl had looked in that big hospital bed when he'd left her there earlier.

She was only in with a broken arm; he couldn't even imagine what it would be like to see her battle a serious illness. To have to have major surgery.

"And that's why you found it hard being with Lucy the other night?" he asked. "Being close to her like that?"

Sophie raised her eyes and her shoulders.

"It wasn't only that though, Lark."

He thought about walking around to her side of the table, reaching across to touch her, to comfort her, but he didn't. He didn't know what to do.

Now there was a waterfall of tears in her eyes that neither he nor she could ignore. Sophie wiped them away. Lark willed his heart to stop beating so hard from watching her pain.

"A long time ago—seven years—before I knew better, I terminated a pregnancy."

He didn't think she would continue, but after a deep breath, she did.

"I was able to forget about it for a long time, but after…"

Lark didn't know what to say. What to think. How to feel.

Sophie caught her breath.

"Everything just caught up to me, and suddenly those seven years seemed like seven weeks or seven days. It felt like only yesterday that I'd made that horrible decision. And if there is anything I could change about my life, it would be that. I'd give up everything else if it meant I could be a mother."

He wasn't going to judge her—decisions like that had to be made by women in difficult situations every day—but it was still hard to hear. Hard to know how to respond.

And he knew firsthand how rewarding it was to be a parent. A life without being a father, without Lucy, wasn't something he could even comprehend.

"In the last couple of years I've had some, ah, female health problems, and in the end I had to have a hysterectomy. A few months ago," she said, the words coming out so fast it almost sounded as if she was relieved to have told him. "I'll never, ever have the chance to be a parent, and I'll never forgive myself."

There was nothing he could say. She wasn't crying, although tears were still shining in her eyes. Emotion had leaked steadily through her voice, made her crack, but she was keeping herself together. In check.

And he felt heartless.

Not because he didn't feel for her now. But because of what he'd thought, what he'd *presumed* the other night. He'd lumped her into the same category as his ex-wife, thought that she was shallow and callous, when in fact she'd been battling something greater than he could ever have imagined.

"Sophie, I don't know what to say," he said, being as honest as he could.

She gave him a sad smile. "There's nothing you *can* say, Lark. That's the problem. There's nothing anyone can do. I'm living with a decision I made, and there were consequences I wasn't prepared for."

"But you can't blame yourself. You obviously had your reasons at the time."

She raised her eyes. "I was twenty-four years old, and the med student in me said that it was only a fetus. That it wasn't a *child* yet, and that it would be better off without me as a mother. That I shouldn't give up my own dreams or bring a child into the world without a father." She laughed, almost hysterically, to herself. "And now I have to live with that decision forever."

Lark stood up, walked around the table, placed a hand on her shoulder. She didn't shrug it away, but he had a feeling she wasn't ready to be comforted. That whatever she was feeling was hard enough to talk about, let alone to connect with someone else over.

"I wish I'd known, Sophie," he said, taking both their plates into the kitchen to give her some breathing space. "I'm so protective over Lucy sometimes that I don't think beyond my own needs."

She turned her chair around, facing him as he rinsed the dishes.

"What do you mean?"

He let the hot water run over the plates before he answered. He hadn't been this honest with another human being since... he couldn't remember when. But she'd opened up to him, talked about something that must have been difficult to get off her chest. He owed her the same. Or maybe he didn't *owe* her. He just felt it was the right time to say something, to be real with her, too.

"Back in California, I was on the rodeo circuit all season," he explained. "I would tour for months, I won plenty of championships, and I ended up with the classic trophy wife."

He watched her face, saw she seemed interested.

"I don't mean to put my ex down, at the time she was everything I'd dreamed of in a woman. Beautiful, outgoing and always the life of the party." He paused, trying not to get sucked back into the memories of their marriage becoming a train wreck. "We had Lucy, everything seemed perfect, and we had more money than we needed and a great lifestyle. But it wasn't until I had the fall that ended my career that the cracks in our marriage really became apparent."

Sophie stood up and walked back into the kitchen. She leaned against the counter, listening to him, making him feel better about talking. Knowing that she wanted to hear.

"What happened?"

Lark shut the dishwasher and braced his frame against the cabinetry.

"As soon as I wasn't famous, once all the attention about my injury died down, Kate became disinterested. Didn't care how heartbroken I was at giving up what I loved. She liked being the celebrity wife, and all I wanted was to settle down on a ranch and try to enjoy my retirement. Spend time with her and Lucy. I'd made more than enough money for us to be comfortable forever and just enjoy being a family."

"But she didn't want that?"

He tried not to sneer at the thought of Kate wanting anything like that.

"She liked to spend money and party with the right people," he told Sophie. "Lucy and I were suddenly a burden, and I filed for divorce. I was going to take her to court for joint custody, but she gave her daughter up like an unwanted puppy, and now she's already engaged to be married to some other poor guy."

"Lark, I'm so sorry. That's terrible."

He shook his head, perhaps too fiercely. Could feel the fire in his eyes. "No, it's life. I should never have married her. But you know what? If I hadn't, I wouldn't have Lucy, and she means everything to me."

He regretted the forcefulness of his words when he saw a flash of pain cross Sophie's face. Knew now that she'd do anything to have her own little Lucy.

"So I worry about her getting close to another person. I keep her away from harm's reach at all times and protect her, don't like the idea of anyone new coming into her life that could make her feel unsettled or hurt her."

Sophie sighed. "And I walked out on you, after you let me in."

"Yeah," he agreed, his voice low. "Yeah, you did. But she was so darn excited about the puppy I don't think she even realized how strange your exit was."

Sophie looked uncomfortable again, as though she wasn't sure what to do.

"Speaking of the puppy, where is he?"

She looked more relaxed, pleased the subject had changed. "He's with my mom for the day," she told him. "And speaking of that, I really should phone and tell her…"

A sudden noise startled Lark, followed by the lights in the house shutting off and the television shuddering to a halt.

The house was suddenly pitch-black, a deathly dark blanket descending upon the room, over the entire interior.

Heavens!

He felt a hand in his.

Sophie must have moved fast.

"What happened?" she whispered, her hand hovering against his forearm.

"Snow must have taken the power out," he said, trying to think logically about what he should do yet distracted by the soft touch of the woman beside him.

"Oh."

He laughed. "I guess that puts an end to the hot shower I was about to offer you."

Sophie tucked tighter against him as a soft bang echoed outside.

"What was that?"

He turned his body half toward her, letting his arm tuck against her back, drawing her slightly against him. He shouldn't have touched her, but she'd initiated it and now he couldn't help himself. Not the way he was feeling right now. Protective in a way, conscious of what she'd been through and how thoroughly she'd listened to him. The way they'd both opened up to one another.

"Everything's magnified because there's no noise inside now," he said. "It's just the weather raging outside."

"Do you have a generator?" she asked, not moving away even as he went to take a step.

It really was pitch-black. He could make out her outline but little else.

"No," he replied, pleased she couldn't see his grimace. It was something he'd meant to look into and had completely forgotten about. "But I do have flashlights and candles handy."

She leaned into him and followed him as he walked.

"Well, that's a start, I guess."

"At least we've eaten. Rustling up something cold might have been harder."

Sophie laughed, but didn't let go of him. It was comforting, having her near.

Lark was about to offer her a sweater, go upstairs and find warmer clothes for them both, but then… He didn't want to stop thinking about Lucy, to stop worrying about her, but was it so bad that he also wanted to think about Sophie? That he wanted to show her that she meant something to him? That she didn't have to be miserable, suffering because of her decisions forever.

"There is another way we could get warm without power."

"How?"

"Our outdoor bath."

He tried not to laugh as her hold on him turned to a grip for a second. Then she let go.

Even if she turned him down, at least he'd taken her mind off the power outage. And his mind off the fact that he'd had to leave his little girl for the night, and there was nothing he could do about it until morning.

"An outdoor bath?" Sophie didn't know what to say.

If tonight could get any stranger, it just had.

She'd never talked to anyone as candidly as she had to Lark. Didn't know how that emotion, those feelings, had spiraled from her mouth as though she'd been holding them close, desperate to spill them.

"It's on the edge of the garden, over the fence in the field," he told her, still standing near even though she'd let go. "I can light the fire and have it steaming-hot pretty quick."

She hoped Lark couldn't hear the way her heart was thudding. Sophie tried to play it cool, not wanting to let on that she was terrified of being alone with him, in the dark, outside. Let alone in a bath.

"You can light it even in the snow?"

Lark's hand found hers, his skin connecting to hers.

"I have a small propane tank out there. One flick of the switch and the fire beneath the bath ignites."

She could imagine how nice it would be. The cool air surrounding them, snow falling and a steaming-hot bath out in the open. It sounded…idyllic. And it would take her mind off everything that was troubling her.

But was she brave enough?

"I don't think I'm up for skinny-dipping." *Ever.*

Lark laughed, but not in a way that belittled her or made fun of her. She relaxed before he even answered.

"Well, I don't think you'll fit anything of Lucy's, and I don't have any women's bathing suits in my wardrobe, but I'm thinking you could either get in before me so I can't see anything, or you could wear your underwear."

She blushed. Even in the dark, she could feel the heat in her cheeks and was pleased he couldn't see her face.

"You won't leave me out there in the pitch-black, or try to scare me, will you?"

"Scared of the dark?" he asked.

She laughed. It sounded scaredy-cat even to her ears. Like a high-pitched bell being tinkled.

"A little."

Then he moved his fingers and she realized they were still palm to palm.

She hated that it felt so good, that she didn't want him to let go.

Hated and loved it at the same time.

"So what do you say?"

She was about to say no, but something made her say otherwise. Something compelled her to disagree with the rational part of her brain.

"Okay."

"Okay?" he questioned her.

"Just don't let go of my hand."

He didn't reply, simply held her hand more firmly, fingers linking with her own.

"Let's get the flashlights and go."

Sophie leaned against the fence post, chanting inside her own head. He'd left her. But then he hadn't really had a choice and she didn't want to go marching off after him. He'd wanted to quickly check on the stabled horses, and she was left watching the water slowly heat up.

The snow was still falling, only lightly now, but still it left a blanket of white in its wake. She'd heard the odd whinny of a horse from the stables, had listened to something rustle far too close and was now shivering, even though she was tucked up in Lark's big jacket.

"Just me," he called.

She shone the light toward his voice, jumping as something rustled nearby.

"I'm not thinking this was such a great idea."

He chuckled and reached for her.

They stood there, close but not touching. She wished they were. His body against hers made her feel that nothing could happen to her, that she'd be safe.

It was a feeling she wasn't used to, not having ever let a man close enough before. She'd always been so determined to be independent and stand on her own two feet.

Right now though, there was something nice about feeling she could depend on Lark, even if it was just for the evening.

He bent down—she could see because she kept the light trained on him—checking the fire. It glowed red with a bluish tinge, more magical when she flicked off the light and watched it in the dark. The big old cast-iron bath was near a water trough, a freshwater pipe feeding into it.

"I'll leave it going on low, but it should be warm enough to get in," he told her.

She kept watching, nervous all over again about getting in, even if she did have to admit that there was something special about a hot bath in the snow.

"Where do we put our clothes?"

"I'll turn around while you strip off, then stow your things in the tree here." He turned his own flashlight on and showed her the hidden cubby within the tree. "Promise I won't look."

She felt to make sure the water was hot enough, then took off her clothes and tapped Lark on the shoulder, passing them to him. She slipped into the piping-hot water, not caring whether it might be too warm for fear of him seeing her. She was still wearing her bra and panties, but she didn't want him shining the light her way and getting an eyeful.

She should have turned her own head away once he'd put her clothes in the tree, but she didn't. Instead, Sophie slid deep into the bath, savoring the hot water on her skin in contrast to the icy air still hitting her cheeks.

And she watched.

Even in the dark her eyes had started to adjust, so while she couldn't see a lot, she could make out Lark's outline. The silhouette of his body, the height of him.

She wondered for a moment if he'd go bare, but looked away before she could find out.

She shouldn't even be thinking like that, no matter how tempting he was. Even if she had explained herself to him, drained herself emotionally by telling him what she'd done in her past, it still didn't mean anything could happen between them.

"I would have lit candles but I doubt they'd last a minute."

Sophie turned back toward his voice, breath catching in her throat as she looked at him standing before her.

Candles she did not need. In fact, nothing else could make this feel even more romantic than it already did.

He eased himself into the water. She could make out his smile as he leaned back opposite her. Their legs touched, brushed, but there was no room to move away so she left hers still, even though they quivered against his in the hot water, made her feel flushed all over, her skin heating even more than it was already.

Lark was watching her—she could feel his eyes on her before she could make them out.

"I told you it was good out here."

Yeah, it was definitely good. "So strange having such a warm body and such a cold face."

They sat there, motionless and silent. Sophie didn't know where to look or what to say. In a way it felt too intimate being here with Lark. And on the other hand, it seemed absolutely right.

Fingers brushed hers. The gentlest of touches.

It almost took her breath away.

Lark was still watching her, waiting for her to react. She didn't do anything, *couldn't,* to start with. But then she wiggled one finger back, then another.

He took her palm, lightly, tugging her toward him.

"Sophie."

The word was only a whisper, but she couldn't ignore it. It was the only word said against a background of dead silence, of wilderness surrounding them.

Somehow she let him draw her closer. As far forward as he could move her within the confines of the bath.

"Turn around," he ordered, voice low.

She wriggled, shoulders coming out of the water, conscious that he might see her wet lace bra.

He pulled her back toward him, so her body was cupped against his. Lark didn't touch her with his hands now, instead he let his arms rest on the rim of the bath, but his legs were on either side of hers, and her back was against his torso.

She knew what he was doing. He was waiting for her to make a move, for her to decide whether she was relaxed enough, ready to be that intimate.

She wasn't, but she did it anyway. Pressed back into him, her skin against his beneath the water, letting her head fall back, to nestle into the space against his chest and beneath his collarbone.

Sophie had sunk lower in the water, and it made her fit against him just right.

They still hadn't said anything to one another, but the silence felt comfortable. As if it would be wrong to break the moment, the feeling that a spell had been cast over them, by saying anything.

Lark's arms slowly moved from the edge of the bath, his hands sliding into the water and landing on her thighs. Gently, so gently. One moved up her torso, landing on her stomach, the other stayed on her leg.

Sophie leaned back farther into him, her head on the side. And then Lark's lips found her skin. His mouth touched her neck, the side of it that was above the water.

A shudder traced through every inch of her body, but she was powerless to move away. Didn't want him to stop.

Ever.

His lips caressed her skin, softly worked their way down her neck and over her shoulder. His fingers were now gliding against her, tickling and teasing her.

"Lark," she said, not knowing why but feeling she had to slow things down.

"Mmm," he murmured against her skin.

"Lark, I think…"

"Don't think," he whispered.

She pulled away, enough so that his mouth fell away from her.

"Are you sure? I mean, you've just come out of a marriage, I've got, well…"

"Sophie?"

She sighed. "Yes."

"Shut up and kiss me."

She gulped. "But…"

Lark wasn't standing for her chatter, for her trying to distract him with her reasons why they shouldn't.

He turned her again in the bath, made her face him this time, moving forward so that her legs could wrap around his torso.

Sophie felt that they were moving too fast, becoming too intimate, even though she wanted it so badly. He held her there before doing anything, arms looped about her, holding her, making her feel secure.

And then he leaned forward, bent his head, took her lips so softly that they were barely touching.

All reason, all argument, fled her mind. She lost herself to the way he felt pressed to her, the hardness of his body in contrast to the silky caress of the water.

Her shoulders were bare, exposed to the cold around them, but she didn't care. Couldn't feel anything other than Lark's lips on hers, especially as they became more insistent, more urgent.

He pulled away only enough to whisper, "Any more arguments?"

Sophie shook her head. It was the only response she was capable of.

"Good."

This time Lark dropped a single kiss to her lips before working his way down her neck, tracing her collarbone, lips dipping almost into the water before moving up the other side of her neck. Then back to her lips, taking her mouth in a kiss that left her feeling drained, incapable of anything other than moving her mouth in time against his.

If he didn't have such a tight hold on her, she might have slipped beneath the water.

Instead, she lost herself to his touch and started to explore. Felt the hard muscles of his back, the strength of his broad shoulders. Reveled in how male and masculine he felt.

"What do you say we head inside?" he asked her, lips whispering across her skin.

She shook her head, suddenly feeling braver than she had earlier.

"No."

"No?"

She pushed him back against the edge of the bath, hands to his chest, moving her legs so she was straddling him, knees planted on either side of him in the deep bath.

CHAPTER FOURTEEN

Lark almost slipped beneath the water he was so surprised. He looked up at Sophie above him, her eyes a level higher than his as she sat on top of him. Her arms were draped across his shoulders, her thighs against his, wrapped around the outside of his legs.

He let out a deep, shuddering breath.

Wow.

When he'd suggested a bath, he hadn't let his mind wander this far. Or at least not *this* far.

He'd kissed her thinking he was pushing his luck, thinking she'd probably shove him away. But there was something about being out here in the dark, with the freezing-cold weather surrounding them, tucked in their own little slice of warm heaven…

This was what he wanted—to keep his mind on Sophie and nothing else. He didn't want to think about his little girl when there was nothing he could do to help her. But this, this was what he wanted.

What he wanted right now was Sophie.

He let her push his head back with one hand, didn't resist as she took control and kissed him. As she set the pace.

Even if he'd wanted to he couldn't have stopped her. Her body fit so snugly to his, her breasts—covered by her soaking-wet bra—skimming against his chest.

"Lark, I'm sorry for walking out on you the other night," she whispered into his neck.

The other night? He couldn't have cared less. He just wanted her lips on his again. Her lips anywhere so long as they were touching *him* somewhere.

He didn't want to be a bad father, would have walked away from even *this* if he'd been able to be at the hospital, but he didn't want to feel guilty for being with Sophie. Not when there was nothing he could do for Lucy until morning.

"You're forgiven," he told her, realizing she was waiting for him to answer.

She took up on his mouth again, before pressing light, feathery kisses to his forehead, then his eyelids, then his nose.

He groaned deep in his throat, wanting to stay submissive beneath her yet finding it so hard. He was desperate to grab her and pin her down with his weight. To explore her body, to touch her, rather than let her have her wicked way with him.

They both had their underwear on, but he couldn't imagine feeling closer to her. It was as if they were bare, skin to skin, their bodies made to fit.

"Kiss me," she ordered, hovering her mouth above his once more.

He didn't need to be asked twice. Lark pushed his arms from the water, taking hold of her face, one hand tangled in her hair, tugging her forward. She landed harder against his chest, her entire body over his, as he took control of her mouth and kissed her over and over again until they were both breathless.

"Sophie," he managed to croak, pulling away from her to speak.

She looked up at him with lazy eyes, a hooded expression on her face. His eyes had adjusted enough now to see well, and he enjoyed her happy, lazy expression.

"Yeah?" she mumbled.

"I think we should go inside."

He didn't say what he wanted. That it was time to drag her to his bed. But she knew what he meant.

He watched as her eyes widened, then softened.

"Okay."

Lark gave her a gentle kiss, rubbing his lips softly against hers, before lifting her and pushing her to the other end of the bath. He got out, ignoring the freezing blast of cold on his hot, wet feet, and raced to the nearby tree. It was only a few feet away but the cold was almost unbearable. He slipped his feet into his boots, grabbed one of the oversize towels he'd brought out, and tucked another towel and her shoes beneath his arm.

He passed them to her, turning his back as she wrapped herself, giving her a moment to emerge from the water as he retrieved their clothes then turned off the gas.

Sophie was wrapped tightly in the towel, and he flicked on his flashlight to light the way.

"Quick, before you get frostbite."

She didn't need any encouragement, trotting along quickly beside him.

Lark moved fast too, but not from the cold. He couldn't have cared if the temperature dropped even lower. All he wanted was to get her inside and pay her back for all that teasing in the bath.

Sophie's entire body was shaking. Her teeth were chattering, the tiny hairs on her arms standing on end, her face burning from the sting of icy air.

She hurried inside when Lark opened the door for her, rushing into the living room after she kicked off her shoes and making for the fire.

It was still burning, embers glowing red, but it needed attention to get it roaring back to life again.

Lark was by her side within an instant, towel now secured around his middle, bending to throw more logs on. She admired his muscular frame as he moved, drinking in the sight of his tanned, golden skin. The pull and release of his shoulder and bicep muscles.

She looked away before he could turn and catch her.

"Are you still cold?" he asked, finished with tending the fire.

Sophie shook her head. The light from the fire made them visible to one another, but the way the fire started to lick up the fresh timber made shadows dance.

He stood up anyway, reaching for the thick throw at the end of the sofa and putting it beside her.

"Here, this will keep you warm."

His voice was low, deep and sexy. She doubted she'd ever tire of that almost-lazy cowboy drawl.

Sophie shuffled closer to him. To wrap herself in the throw would mean ditching the damp towel, and she wasn't sure if she was ready to do that.

She gasped as Lark took charge, moving on his knees toward her and slowly slipping the towel from her shoulders, exposing them, before forcing the towel down lower until it was sitting at her waist.

Then he took hold of her body, hands on her bare skin, and pressed her gently down onto the throw.

Sophie let him, nervous, but at the same time exhilarated. Wanting his hands on her, desperate for his touch.

She forgot about her soaking-wet underwear and relaxed beneath his touch. Lark took her hands and pinned them above her head in his one big hand, the other resting on her belly, where his lips soon followed. He traced a path up her skin, skimming across her breasts as they rose and fell in rapid succession, inching his way up her chest and neck, until his body covered hers and he kissed her full on the mouth.

"I'm starting to like power-outs," he whispered.

Sophie sighed, lost to his touch. "Me, too," she said back.

Lark feathered his kisses across her face, down her shoulder and arm, stopping at her wrist.

"I want you, Sophie."

She mumbled something even *she* couldn't understand, not sure what to say to him.

"Just say yes," he whispered against her skin.

"Yes," she said on a bubble of air, exhaling deeply.

Lark refocused on her mouth, kissing away any doubt she might have felt. His fingers skimmed her bra strap before slowly slipping it away.

Sophie sighed. Again.

For a girl who was usually scared of the dark, she was coping remarkably well.

Tomorrow, they could deal with reality—the fact that they were both worried about Lucy, going back to the hospital.

But tonight? Tonight she wasn't going to feel guilty about being pleasured in a way she'd never experienced before.

CHAPTER FIFTEEN

SOPHIE woke to something tickling her face and the hard frame of a man pressed tightly against her back.

She opened one eye to peek and saw that it was only the faux-fur throw that was touching her cheek before shutting both eyes tight again and willing herself to go back to sleep.

There was time to panic later. Right now, she wanted to enjoy the feel of Lark against her, the way his still-naked body felt against hers, the warmth of his skin, the strength of his arm curled around her protectively even in slumber.

Last night had been…she didn't even know how to explain it. One moment they'd been talking over dinner, discussing things she'd never talked about with anyone, and then they were bare and making love in front of the fire.

Wow.

Sophie turned, knowing sleep wouldn't find her again, not now she was awake and analyzing the night before. She wriggled slowly, turning to face Lark, his arm still around her.

She watched him sleep. The way his lips were parted, dark lashes touching his cheeks. His hair was messy and disheveled, stubble lined his jaw. Her fingers itched to touch, to run along his face and tug through his hair. But she stayed as still as possible, not wanting the moment to end. Or a new moment to begin.

"You're staring."

She jumped in his arms. "Lark!"

His eyes opened in a lazy kind of way. "I could feel you watching me."

She tucked against him, face to his chest, not wanting to brave his eyes yet. "You scared me."

He chuckled, clearing his throat and removing his arm from around her to rub his eyes.

Sophie felt bare all of a sudden. Cold from not having his skin against hers, she wished she could tuck her body against his and snuggle for the rest of the day. Forget everything and stay here with Lark.

She sighed. If only.

"You sound like you've got the world resting on your shoulders."

Sophie wriggled against him again, pleased when he opened his arms back up and enveloped her. "I was thinking that it would be so much easier if we could stay like this for at least today."

"Agreed, if I didn't have horses to feed." He grinned. "And then a little girl to retrieve."

She nodded, refusing to think about anything other than Lark right now. She pressed her lips to his chest, not meaning to tease him but realizing she was by his groan.

"And just like that I've forgotten all about the horses."

Sophie pulled away so that her chest left his. "Don't let me make your animals go hungry."

He tugged her back, his lips finding hers, locking their mouths. She happily gave in to his kiss, enjoying the relaxing way he touched her, how comfortable she felt with him.

A knock echoed out loud and clear through the house.

"Please tell me that wasn't someone knocking at the door."

Lark kissed her one last time before sitting up.

"Who on earth would be here in the snow at this time of morning?" he asked.

Sophie grabbed the blanket and wrapped it around herself, shyly watching as Lark stood up, naked, to search for his clothes.

"Lucky we had the fire going all night—everything's pretty dry."

She averted her eyes as he bent to pull on his things.

"Shall I stay here?"

He nodded and moved down the hall, still doing up his jeans.

"Wrap up and stay here," he called over his shoulder.

She did as he said, suddenly very self-conscious about the fact she was sitting with nothing other than a blanket around her. Her clothes were strewn around the room, but she wasn't brave enough to attempt to get dressed in case the person at the door saw her.

Muffled voices echoed down the hall, but she couldn't hear what was being said. Only that it was another man.

Lark appeared within minutes, looking handsome as ever.

"Local farmer," he said, bracing himself in the doorway. "He's clearing snow away from driveways with his tractor, but he said the road's pretty dangerous from here into town still. They're advising everyone to stay home."

"Lucy," she said, yesterday's events playing back through her head. "Will you manage to get to her?"

Lark looked distant, as though he was focused on something other than her or the conversation they were having. "Yeah, I'll get there. Might take me a while but if I can't drive I'll ride a horse in and bring her home."

Sophie knew she'd lost him now. There was no chance of snuggling back up under the blanket and forgetting the day away.

"So you're going out to feed your horses?"

"Yeah," he said, looking back at her and crossing the room, his eyes searching hers out as though he'd been momentarily distracted and was now connected again. "Want to come?"

She smiled up at him, pleased to be included. "Can we drink coffee first?"

He bent to kiss her before retrieving her clothes and putting them beside her. "I'll make an exception this once," he told her. "You get dressed. I'll find a warm coat for you and get coffee started."

Sounded good to her.

Lark's head was full of too many thoughts. He was stressing about Lucy being at the hospital for so long, guilty about the night he'd spent while she'd been alone. But he would never have left her if he'd been allowed to stay, and it was still too early for her to be discharged. It wasn't that he wanted to leave Sophie— heavens only knew he'd stay curled up with her in his arms for days on end if he could—but he had to bring Lucy home. She'd hate being there alone, wondering where he was. He already felt guilty enough about leaving her there for the night.

And he had to do the rounds outside, check that the horses had fared okay through the night and give them all more hay.

He turned from pouring coffee as Sophie cleared her throat behind him. She looked beautiful, as she always did, but the gentle flush in her cheeks and the shine in her eyes made his heart race even more than usual.

Last night had been...incredible. Completely unexpected.

He dropped the spoon into the cup he'd been about to stir and walked toward her, stopping only when he reached her to press a kiss to her forehead, then her lips. He drew her into his body, wrapping his arms around her.

"Hey," he said.

She nestled tighter into him.

"I'm sorry we couldn't stay like that for longer."

He felt her nod against him. "Me, too," she mumbled.

"Promise I'll make it up to you, okay?"

He didn't know how, but he was sure there were plenty of ways he could.

"Coffee?"

Sophie stepped back. "White, one sugar."

He squeezed her hand before going back to pour her a cup. "Coming right up."

* * *

They walked their coffees out the back door with them, sipping at the piping-hot liquid as they strolled.

"At least it's not snowing anymore."

Lark led the way, walking a step ahead of her. "You sure you're warm enough?"

"I'm fine, stop worrying about me."

He walked into the stable before her and she couldn't help but laugh at the neighing that ensued when he called out "Good morning."

"They know who Dad is, right?"

He glanced back over his shoulder, grinning. "Sure do."

Lark marched down toward the first stall, stopping to talk to the horse she recognized from the other day, Cougar. Then he moved on, calling out as he went and emerging from an open stall with an armful of hay. She stood and watched as he went back and forth between the stalls, each time with hay.

"You all right waiting while I muck out their stables?"

She spied a large empty bucket, upturned it and sat down. "Sure am."

Sophie finished her coffee as she watched him work and listened to him talk to the horses.

"Do you think they know what you're saying?" she called out.

Lark's head appeared over the door. "Maybe not, but they're very good at pretending."

She thought of her own animal then, the little puppy. Sam, as Lucy had named him.

Just being here with Lark made her think about giving him the dog all over again.

"You know the puppy?" she asked.

"Yeah," Lark called out.

"Were you serious about getting a dog for Lucy?"

He appeared again, this time pushing a barrow full of sawdust and horse manure. "Why, you thinking of giving yours away for sure?"

Lark stood, leaning against the stable door and stroking his horse when he stuck his head out to see what was going on.

"I am actually."

"Why? He seemed like a nice pup."

"He is, but I can't offer him the sort of life that you and Lucy can," she explained. "If he stays with me, I have to take him back to the city with me when I go back, and I work such long hours. It's not really fair."

A darkness crossed Lark's face, made his eyes change, but he didn't say anything. He just stood, watching her as though he was waiting for her to say something else.

"So what do you say?" she asked.

He shrugged. "I'd say that the last thing I need is something else to look after right now, but Lucy is desperate and we probably both know that I'm inclined to say yes to her. Over something like this, anyway."

She was sad at the thought of giving Sam up, but thinking about the way the dog had played with Lark's daughter and the farm he'd have to run around on, told her it was the right thing.

"So you'll take him?"

He walked back down the row of stalls and went into another, calling out as he moved. "If you're absolutely sure, but I think you should take your time. You know, deciding."

She stood up and followed. "I've had enough time to think about it."

She watched him move around the stall, careful not to disturb the horse as he worked. It didn't take him long.

"You want to know what I think?" he asked.

Maybe. Maybe not.

But she was curious about what he was going to say.

"Shoot."

He pushed out the barrow again. "I think, from what you told me last night, that you're not sure about anything right now. Am I right?"

Sophie bit down on her lower lip. What she wasn't sure

about was having this conversation with him, or with anyone for that matter.

"I think you're unhappy with your life in general, and you're at a crossroads of sorts. Like I was," he said. "You don't really want to go back to your job, but you feel you have to, and you're not happy here, either. You don't feel like you fit in anywhere right now, and your guilt is eating at you from the inside."

She swallowed, more than once, trying to ignore what he was saying. Her eyes were starting to burn as if she was about to cry, but she wouldn't let herself. She was too strong to break down like that in front of him.

"So am I right?"

She wasn't going to admit that he was anything close to right, even if he was.

"What is it you suggest I do, then, since you claim to know me so well?" she asked, hearing the frostiness of her own voice.

He looked hesitant, uncertain about the blunt way she'd replied.

"I was wondering if maybe you want to be back here, at home in Queenstown, but you don't know what you'd do here. Don't want to give up the life and job you've worked so hard for," he said. "Maybe you should open up a practice here, explore another field as a doctor."

"Give up surgery?" she asked, incredulous.

Lark let his shoulders rise then fall. She wanted to curse at him, yell at him and tell him to mind his own bloody business. But she didn't want to show him that he'd hit a nerve, or have an argument. Not when he was so close to the truth.

The thing was, it had crossed her mind, but she wasn't ever going to give up surgery. Couldn't. She owed it to herself not to, and she sure wasn't going to do it because a man suggested it.

But at the same time, spending time with Lucy had made her think that maybe she couldn't *not* have children in her life. As hard as it was, she'd be lost without the smiling little faces she'd become so accustomed to seeing each day in her job. To the good she could do.

Even if there was pain to deal with, baggage that came with what she'd been through and what had happened to her in the past.

"You know what? What do I know," Lark said, surprising her, reaching out to touch her arm before moving off to finish his work. "All I can say is that it would be nice if you were around, you know, permanently."

She went back to sit on the bucket.

Him wanting her around was exactly what she'd been afraid of.

Lark rode down the snow-covered road at a slow, steady walk. If he'd waited another few hours, he might have been able to use the car, but he doubted it. And the local farmer might have come back for him, but he didn't have time to wait around. He'd waved goodbye to Sophie, saddled up Cougar and headed for town.

The horse had a blanket folded over his rump to keep him warm, and he had extra-warm clothes for Lucy tucked in a bag. They'd make a sight arriving at the hospital, but he didn't care. He wanted his girl up in the saddle in front of him, then tucked up in her own bed.

Then he'd be happy.

Make that, he was already happy. This was simply the final piece of the puzzle.

He couldn't believe how wrong he'd been, judging Sophie like that. She was exactly the kind of woman he'd originally thought her to be. More deeply troubled than he could have imagined, but still genuine. Kind.

The type of woman he wished he'd met years ago.

He'd never believed for a moment that he could find a woman he might one day want to bring into Lucy's life permanently. And now maybe he had.

The only problem was that she'd be leaving.

He wished she'd decide to stay, but it seemed unlikely. Although he wasn't averse to seeing how things worked out long-distance before they figured something out...

Lark stopped himself. That was getting *way* ahead.

They'd only just spent the night together. Only known each other how long? He needed to slow things down, remember what his priorities were. Take this nice and steady.

So why was he feeling that he'd finally met his soul mate and had to do anything to make the relationship work?

She was on the verge of hyperventilating.

Sophie paced back and forth, eyes on the window, feeling trapped. She needed to get out of here. Didn't want to be here still when Lark returned, even though she'd kissed him good-bye and told him she'd wait.

Last night had been incredible, magical, but she was starting to panic. She needed space, because suddenly she could see her life before her, see the mistakes she'd already made and the ones she could so easily make now—if she didn't do the right thing.

Her own mother had given everything up for a man, and it was something Sophie had always said she wouldn't do. She'd never give up her dreams for a man. Or for anyone else for that matter.

And it wasn't that Lark had asked her to do it for him, but she knew he wanted her to stay. He'd said as much. Suggested she give up her life, walk away from what she'd worked so hard to achieve to move back here.

At least her mother had had a family. She had given up her own dreams of becoming a veterinary surgeon, had married young, then had children. But that was the missing piece of the puzzle for Sophie.

If she gave everything up for a man, she still couldn't have a family of her own. Would Lark really want her in his life, long-term, as anything more than a fling, if she couldn't have his children when he clearly loved being a dad so much?

When her father had walked out on her mother, at least her mother had had *something*. She could hold her head high, and no matter what, she could look at her children and be proud of her role as a mother.

Sophie only had her career. It was too important to her to give it up.

So why was she thinking that what Lark had suggested wasn't so ridiculous after all?

And why was she thinking that having a child like Lucy in her life might make up for not being able to love a child of her own?

A noise made her look up, stop pacing.

The farmer was back.

She ran to the door and threw it open. "Hi."

He tipped his hat and climbed down from the tractor cab.

"You still okay here?" he called out.

She smiled and walked out. "You're not heading near town, are you?"

He gave her a wink. "Close enough. I can give you a ride most of the way."

Sophie smiled and gave him a thumbs-up before running back inside, grabbing a pair of wellies and closing the door behind her.

She knew Lark would be upset to find her gone, but she had to go. She couldn't stay here and feel suffocated any longer.

She had to go.

Sophie hated that she was always running from Lark, but she couldn't stop herself.

She couldn't torture herself by thinking that she could ever mean anything to Lucy. Not as more than a fun babysitter.

She would never be her mother, just like she'd never be a mother to her own children.

There was no point pretending otherwise and breaking her heart all over again in the process.

CHAPTER SIXTEEN

LARK opened the door and carried Lucy inside.

"I can walk," Lucy said, giggling as he held her tighter.

"You might be able to walk but I want to carry you."

Even if it did hurt his back a touch, he didn't care.

She wriggled, but not hard. If he'd really believed she wanted to be put down he would have done so, but she seemed pretty happy tucked in his arms.

He was about to call out, to see where Sophie was, but something felt off to him. He'd been gone for a few hours—surely she would have been waiting for them, listening out. And he couldn't hear any noise in the house.

The silence annoyed him.

He'd expected to come home to a woman in his house. To a smile and a kiss, to open arms even, and instead all he was hearing was silence.

Anger started to gnaw its way through his gut, but he forced it away. He had Lucy back home and that was what mattered right now.

"Can I go to my room?"

He dropped her gently to her feet. "Sure thing, kiddo. You hungry?"

"Nah," she said, bouncing off down the hallway.

"Careful of that arm!"

She ignored him, or pretended to anyway.

"I'm going to go put Cougar back in his stable. I'll be back in soon, okay?"

"Yep!" she hollered back.

He went to the back door, pulled on his boots and went to retrieve the horse he'd left tethered to the post.

Lark didn't have to look around to know Sophie wasn't here. There was no sign of her and he could just *feel* that she'd gone.

He wanted to give her the benefit of the doubt, but after she'd run out on him last time? He had a feeling the same thing had happened again.

Lark forced himself to smile as he approached his horse, not wanting the animal to think he was angry with him.

Inside he simmered with a rage that was hard to ignore, a burning flare of pain that told him what an idiot he'd been.

He'd given her a second chance, acknowledged that he'd been wrong to judge her when she'd fled the other night. But if she'd run out on him again, he didn't know if he could be quite so forgiving. He was starting to see a pattern and he didn't like it.

Even if she had been through hell and back recently, there was no excuse for walking out like that.

Lark led the horse to the stable, wanting to get the job over with so he could pummel his fist into something and curse before joining his daughter back inside.

He'd thought last night had meant something. That even though Sophie might not be hanging around for good, that they had something. Something real. Something he had doubted he'd ever find.

Something he hadn't even known he'd been yearning for.

How wrong he'd been.

"Sam!"

Sophie called out to the puppy, trying her hardest to sound perky. It wasn't easy, but she'd learned enough since she'd been helping at the shelter to know that dogs responded best to upbeat and happy.

"Come. Sam, *come*," she commanded.

The puppy continued to run laps around her, tongue and ears flapping in the wind.

Sophie was starting to realize that she wasn't particularly skilled in the art of animal-training.

She winced as her phone rang again. She checked the caller identification.

Lark.

Again.

He'd already called once before, and she'd ignored it. And she was about to do the same again. She couldn't face talking to him. Didn't know what to say.

She wished she hadn't run out, yet she knew it had been the only option she had.

Except for maybe staying to confront him. Admitting that the night before had probably been a mistake. Telling him that she wasn't prepared to change her life for him. Or for any man.

Sophie groaned and dropped to the ground, lying flat-out on the still-damp grass. She no longer cared.

"Argh!"

She raised her hands to shield her face as a pink tongue swept back and forth across her skin.

"Sam!"

She managed to push herself up into a sitting position, the puppy clambering all over her and trying to sit on her knee.

"So that's all I had to do to get you to come, huh?"

The dog wagged his tail some more and tried to lick her face again.

"I do love you, mister, but I still think you'd be better off on a farm."

He cocked his head to the side, looking at her with what she could only imagine was a curious expression on his face.

"I know, all you want to do is play, right?"

Sophie reached for her phone, switched it off, then got up to find the ball they'd been playing with earlier.

Anything to take her mind off the man she couldn't stop moping over.

Lark dropped Lucy off at school and started the drive back to the farm. He'd almost kept her home, but she'd put her hand on her hip and told him it was only a broken arm, and he'd had to agree.

He couldn't shield her from everything, not forever. Even if that did mean she was going to gather some bumps and bruises, be hurt every now and again. She was a kid, and he had to deal with it.

He gripped the wheel a little tighter as he thought about what else he wasn't dealing with particularly well.

Sophie.

She was driving him mad. Or it was more that her absence was driving him mad.

It had been two days since the snowstorm. Two long days since she'd walked out on him. Again.

He'd called her a few times, trying to ignore his anger and telling himself that he was only attempting to make contact to check she was all right. That she'd gotten home okay.

Then he'd called her the last time wanting to give her a piece of his mind.

He was pleased she hadn't answered *that* call.

But each time he'd tried then failed to get hold of her, he'd known she was avoiding him. That she didn't want to hear from him. And although he hated to admit it, knowing she had run out on him hurt.

Like hell.

Lark pulled up the driveway, traveling slowly, and drove his truck around the side so he could unload some supplies into the barn.

He looked up as he hefted a sack of grain, eyes skimming the old bath on the edge of the field.

Lark looked away.

But then he saw the rescue horses he'd been caring for.

And he realized what he had to do.

If he wanted an explanation, wanted to talk to her and find out what the hell had happened and what was going on, he only had to use the horses as a ploy.

She cared too much not to come if she thought something had happened to them. If she thought something was wrong.

It might be a dirty trick, but then her running out on him hadn't been exactly aboveboard, either.

He picked up his mobile and called the animal shelter.

Two could play at this game.

The last thing Sophie wanted was to explain to her work colleagues why she was avoiding Lark.

"So you need me to go now?"

Elisabeth frowned slightly, as though she didn't mean to but couldn't help it.

"I can go myself if it's a problem," she said. "It's up to you, but Mr. Anderson did sound rather concerned."

Sophie wasn't sure what to do. On the one hand she had every right to refuse. She was only volunteering, whereas Elisabeth was a paid employee.

She dug her nails into the soft skin of her arm.

Now she was starting to be a complete bitch just thinking like that. She was the one who'd offered to volunteer here. If she had to face up to Lark, then face up she would.

"Sophie?"

She shook herself out of her mood. "Of course, I'm sorry," she said. "I've just got a lot on my mind, not concentrating properly."

"Only if you're sure?"

She gave Elisabeth a beamer of a smile and collected her

bag. "I'm fine, honestly. I'll give you a call later and let you know what the situation is."

Sophie didn't even let herself think about where she was going or what she was going to have to confront. The horses were the priority here. Her personal issues with Lark were irrelevant—she simply had to remain professional and hold her head high.

Even if she did still feel guilty about what she'd done.

Again.

Lark had no idea why he was so tied up in knots over Sophie, why she had gotten under his skin and wouldn't go away. No matter how much he'd tried to tell himself over the past few days that she wasn't right for him, that he wasn't ready for a new, serious relationship, he knew it was a lie.

She had some explaining to do, sure. But there was something special between them. Something he couldn't ignore no matter how furious she made him, and he wanted to know the real her. Know why she'd run out on him, *again*.

He ran his fingers over the timber fence, waiting for her to arrive.

What he wanted right now was to hear her out—if she was prepared to talk.

Maybe he was thinking too deeply into the situation. Maybe she just wasn't interested and had run because she regretted the night they'd spent together.

But then maybe she felt the same way he did.

A man could only hope.

CHAPTER SEVENTEEN

As she walked toward Lark, Sophie felt as if there was a troop of butterflies in her stomach, all caught in a cage and trying to escape. Her palms were sweaty, her mouth was dry and all she wanted to do was run.

But this time she wasn't going to. Wouldn't. Because she'd come here as a professional, to do a job, and she owed it to Lark to face up to him. Ignoring his calls had been gutless, even if she hadn't known what to say to him.

She was here now and she was going to act like the grown-up, professional woman that she was.

Sophie made herself smile as she approached him. He was leaning against the post-and-rail fencing, one foot hitched behind him, elbows resting.

As though he didn't have a care in the world.

Except, the glint in his eyes told her otherwise.

"Hi," she called.

Lark raised his head slightly, looking straight at her. "Hi."

She rubbed one hand over her jeans—nervous—and the other gripped her notepad tightly.

"I was told you had a problem here? That something was wrong with one of the…"

Lark stood up straight and walked toward her.

"You won't be needing this," he said, removing the pad from her hand and tucking it into his back pocket.

What? "Lark, the horses? I…"

"This way."

He pressed a hand to the small of her back and forced her to walk forward.

"I really don't have time for this," she grumbled, wondering what he was up to.

"Make time," he said, his voice telling her he was deadly serious about whatever it was he was up to.

She didn't argue with him. Didn't have the strength to.

Or maybe she didn't want to.

"Can you at least tell me what we're doing?"

He pointed toward the stable block. She squinted, straining to see inside.

"What?"

Then she realized. There were two horses saddled up. Waiting. The call in about the horses had been no more than a trick to get her here.

"Oh, no…"

He pressed harder on her back. "Oh, yes."

Sophie tried to stop walking, but he pushed her forward.

"We're going for a ride. No arguments."

"Lark, I can't. I'm sorry, but I can't," her voice was little more than a whisper.

He reached his arm around her waist then, forcing her to spin. To face him.

"You owe me an hour, Sophie," he said, eyes and voice intense. "One hour to explain yourself, and to let me explain myself to you."

She gulped. Tried to focus on the rise and fall of her chest, of her breathing. "No."

He lifted her chin, placed his fingers beneath it to make her look up.

"Is it that you regret what we did? Was it you wishing we'd never spent the night together?" he asked. "Was that why you left? Or is it something else?"

Sophie shook her head. She didn't want to go there.

Lark smiled at her, his face as soft and tender as when he'd held her that night in his arms. When they'd made love.

"Tell me," he said.

This time he didn't touch her back; instead, he took her hand, and she didn't have the heart to pull away.

Because as much as she didn't want to admit it, feeling his hand in hers felt so right.

It always had.

Lark reached for the quiet mare he'd saddled up for Sophie.

"Give me your leg and I'll help you up."

He almost laughed at the serious expression on her face, but he stopped himself. He'd expected more of a fight, but she was being surprisingly obliging.

"Are you sure?"

He beckoned her forward with his hand. "She's quiet as a lamb and you've got good sturdy boots on. You'll be fine." He paused. "And if I wasn't sure I wouldn't be putting you up there."

She looked pained, as if she wanted to say no but couldn't.

"Fine," she grumbled.

Lark bent, held out his hand. She placed her knee in it.

"Like this, right?" she asked.

"Yep, on the count of three."

He was impressed by how easily she sprang up into the saddle, landing with only the softest of thuds.

Lark passed her the reins. "I can keep a rope attached to you, if you want, but she should happily walk along beside me."

Sophie patted the horse on the neck. "Take it just in case."

He turned around to the horse he'd saddled for himself, placed his foot in the stirrup and mounted.

"Let's go."

They rode in silence, walking, for a while. Lark wanted to give Sophie time to think. To be in the saddle, beside him, so he could try to gauge what to say, what to ask her.

He smiled. He hadn't realized that he'd finally stopped pining for rodeo-riding. Stopped thinking about what could have been. He was happy here, and he was thankful at least to still be in a saddle at all.

"Lark, I know I'm going to sound like a broken record, but I am sorry about walking out on you again. Truly I am."

He looked over at her. Watched her face, saw real pain there.

He would do anything to take that ache away. To be there for her.

If she'd only stop running.

"I need to know why, Sophie. Why you left, why you wouldn't answer my phone calls. Why I had to pretend the horses were in trouble before you'd come back to me."

He could see tears welling in her eyes, but he had to ask her. Had to make her give him the answers he needed to hear.

"Sophie, please. I need to know." He could hear how gruff his own voice was, hoped she could tell how much he needed her to be real with him.

"Lark, I don't know what to say to you."

"Just tell me, Sophie. If you didn't regret what happened between us, tell me what it was."

She looked away. He let her. Didn't ask her anything else. Didn't tell her to look at him.

Lark simply waited.

It could never work between them.

She smiled sadly, her eyes damp.

"What do you want from me, Lark? Why are we here?"

He had thought that much would be obvious.

"We're here because I want to know why you walked out on me." He paused. "Because I thought there was something between us, that we could *be* something. And right now you can't even let me in."

He pulled back on the reins lightly, asking his horse to stop. Sophie's mount stopped when his did. He nudged his horse in the side to make him walk closer, so he was beside Sophie.

Lark placed a hand on her thigh, looked into her eyes. "I know you feel it, too."

A large tear plopped down her cheek. He reached to wipe it away, let his finger linger there.

"You don't want me, Lark. Trust me."

He shook his head. "You're wrong," he said, in a voice no louder than a whisper.

She glanced away then back again. "I can't have children, Lark, and that means we won't ever be right for one another, okay?" She shook her head, as if it might rid her body of the guilt and tears. "I did it because I didn't want what happened to my mother to happen to me, or to my child." She gulped back air. "It was one night, one mistaken night, and that means I'll never have a pretty nursery and a crib for my baby, or a happy little family."

Lark forced his fists to soften. "Who says that has to define you, Sophie? Tell me why you can't be happy without that?"

"I can't deal with what you have here, Lark. Your daughter, the fact you obviously love children…"

He waited for her to finish her sentence. She didn't.

"Do you think it bothers me that you can't have children?"

Her eyes looked as though they'd sprung a leak. Tears started to trickle down her cheeks and onto her nose.

"Don't you?"

He jumped from his horse then, landed heavily on the ground.

"Come here," he ordered, reaching for her and helping her to dismount, too.

She landed beside him, her face distraught.

Lark opened his arms and drew her against him, his lips falling to her head. Then he bent, to look into her eyes, to kiss her cheeks, her nose, her forehead. And then her lips.

"I already have a daughter, Sophie. And even if I didn't, that's not what's important here. It's you I want."

He felt pain. Physical, heart-wrenching pain as she took the time to compose herself.

"I've seen the way you are with her, Lark. Why would you want to be with a woman who can't ever give you any more?"

He sighed. "You're who I care about, not some hypothetical children I *might* want in the future."

"But don't you want more children?"

He took a few steps back, turned away. Looked out over his land.

Too late he realized that it was a mistake. That he shouldn't have paused, should have answered her straightaway, because the look on her face showed a broken woman.

"Sophie…"

She shook her head fiercely. "I need to go, Lark. *Please.*"

"Sophie, I didn't mean…"

He'd mucked that up without even meaning to.

She wouldn't meet his eyes. "Take me back."

Lark bent to take her foot, to lift her back into the saddle. He didn't know what else to do.

"Sophie, come back tomorrow," he said, hand still resting on her leg, wanting her to look at him. "I don't care if you can't have children. I don't care what you've done in your past. I just want to give us a chance."

She turned sad eyes toward him, eyes still filled with tears.

"If you're ready to trust me, come back here tomorrow afternoon." He paused. "I'll be waiting."

He could have said what he wanted to say then and there, but there was someone else he had to talk to first. Someone else whose opinion mattered as much as his own.

Until then, he had to keep his mouth shut.

CHAPTER EIGHTEEN

LARK'S heart started to beat so hard he thought it might explode from his chest. She was here. She'd actually come.

He'd hoped. He'd wished. And at times he'd been sure.

But for the past hour or so, he'd thought he'd been wrong.

"Daddy!" Lucy ran around the corner, cheeks flushed bright red. "She's here."

"I know."

He smiled at his daughter, pleased that she was so excited. He'd risked breaking her little heart this morning by letting her get involved, but he felt strongly enough about Sophie to want to make this right. To want to give them a chance.

Sophie rounded the corner and he couldn't help the smile that hit his face. Surely if she'd come, it meant she felt the same way he did. Or at least he hoped.

"You came," he said, his voice laced with gruff emotion.

She looked as though she'd been crying.

"Sophie?"

He pulled her into him, feeling her reluctance but holding her tight anyway. It only took a second for her to wrap her arms around him, sobbing softly as she pressed against his shoulder. His lips fell to her head, he inhaled her sweet fragrance.

Lark wanted so badly to hold her, but he pushed her back, looked into her eyes, hand on her chin.

"Lark…"

He held up one finger to touch her lips. "Shhh."

She didn't make a noise.

"Sophie, a few weeks ago I would have told you I didn't want a relationship again, ever," he told her, voice low. "I thought I'd never want to be close to a woman again. That I'd never be able to trust someone enough ever to let them in, to let them close to me or to Lucy."

She watched him back, eyes shining with emotion.

"And then I met you," he whispered, reaching for her hands, holding them tight in his. "I met you and you changed my mind, just like that."

Her head moved from side to side. "But…"

Lark shook his head, not letting her interrupt.

"I love children, Sophie, but if being with you means that's not in our future, then I don't care."

He could see in her eyes that maybe, just maybe, she was starting to believe him.

Lark closed his eyes for a moment, before pulling Sophie forward. Pulling her against his chest and tipping her head back, going to kiss her then stopping before their lips met.

"Marry me," he whispered, his voice barely audible.

His heart leaped as Sophie looked back at him, wide-eyed. "What?"

"Marry me," he repeated, his voice stronger, more assertive now. "Marry me, Sophie. Promise me you won't walk out again. *Marry me.* Be my wife and be the stepmom to Lucy I know you'd love to be."

She stepped back, her face frozen in an expression he couldn't fathom.

"No."

He grabbed her hand, pulled her back in toward him.

"No?" he asked.

"Lark, you can't just ask me to marry you! I don't even live here permanently. We don't know enough about one another. We…"

"Sophie, I knew from the moment I met you that you were different. If I wasn't sure, I wouldn't have asked you."

She kept shaking her head, but she didn't resist when he kissed her. Her lips moved against his willingly, even though she'd said no to his question.

"Tell me why you won't say yes?"

Her lips were plump, full from being kissed. She didn't pull away from him, but she still hadn't said yes.

"I have a job in Auckland. I'm not just going to give that up because you want to get married. Even if I would consider moving back here, well, I'm not going to be pressured into anything."

He gave her some breathing space. So that was the problem.

"My mother gave up everything to marry my father, Lark. I'm not prepared to do the same."

"I like that you have a career," he said. "We can be together while you're here, figure something out when you have to go back. I've had the relationship that looked perfect on paper, Sophie. If we have to bend the rules a little to make things work between us, then so be it."

Sophie placed her hand on his chest, moved him back, then stood there. Palm still resting on him.

"What if I did move back here for good? What if I did it because I wanted to, not because you suggested it?"

Sophie's head felt like a spinning top. She couldn't think, could barely breathe.

And all she *could* think was that he'd asked her to marry him.

Lark Anderson, the handsome cowboy she'd liked from the moment she'd met him, had asked her to marry him. And now he was trying to talk her into it.

Her heart beat faster. Pounded.

Could I really become part of this beautiful little family and be a mother to Lark's gorgeous child?

"Have you asked Lucy?" she heard herself ask, not wanting to get her hopes up.

Worry clouded her brain like storm clouds before rain.

She couldn't believe she was even discussing this. She should have done what she was good at, what she'd already done to him before, and run. Run like the wind.

But something was keeping her here. Not allowing her to leave. Stopping her from saying no again.

Because she did want to be with Lark. Couldn't believe that he'd worn his heart on his sleeve and told her how he felt, that he was offering her the chance to be a mother. To be stepmom to his precious girl.

"You might not be able to have children of your own, Sophie, but you'll make an excellent stepmom," he paused. "And a beautiful, wonderful wife."

She could have cried. But she didn't let herself. Wouldn't.

Was he serious? How could he feel that way about her when she'd been so rude? So careless with his heart by walking out on him after the night they'd spent together?

"Marry me, Sophie?" he asked again.

"Why?" Her voice was a whisper, a choke now.

She watched as his Adam's apple bobbed. As he swallowed hard.

"Because I think I love you."

He looked so vulnerable, as though he'd been stripped bare of his soul.

She laughed, just a little. She couldn't help it.

It was then that she let herself admit the truth, too.

"I think I love you, too," she whispered.

And she did. She'd known it for sure after the night they'd spent together out under the stars.

He took her face in both his hands, pressed the softest of kisses to her lips.

"I'm not moving because you want me to," she protested, her lips struggling to move away from his.

Lark gave her one of his lazy grins. "I don't care where we live, or what we do, I just want to be with you. And no more running, okay?"

Sophie giggled. "No more running," she agreed.

"Promise?"

"I promise."

Sophie sighed into Lark's mouth as he kissed her, his lips moving against hers. When he pulled away, she couldn't take her eyes off him.

"For the record, I'd already decided not to renew my contract at the hospital."

He raised an eyebrow, eyes trained on hers. "Yeah?"

"I love what I do, Lark, but I need to figure something else out. It's not the right place for me anymore."

"Whatever you decide, I'll be here for you."

She wrapped her arms around his neck. "I know."

"Did she say yes?"

Sophie jumped back as Lucy's excited, high-pitched voice sounded out behind them. Lark swiftly pulled her back to him, arm woven around her waist.

"What do you say about Sam coming to live with us, too?" Lark asked.

Lucy's eyes lit up. "Sam the puppy?"

He laughed. "Yeah, Sam the puppy."

"Cool!"

Lark dropped a kiss to Sophie's head. She felt her face flush, not sure why she was embarrassed, nervous, about him telling his daughter.

"Are you going to be my stepmom, Sophie?"

She laughed, happier than she'd ever been. "I'd love to be, Lucy. More than you could ever imagine, so long as you'll have me."

"So I'll get a dog *and* a stepmom, right?" she asked her father.

Sophie laughed with Lark as he swung his daughter around before placing her on the ground.

"A stepmom and a dog," he repeated.

Sophie bent down to look Lucy in the eye, wanting to be on her level.

"I know it must be hard being without your mom, but I do know what it feels like, Lucy. And I promise I won't leave you."

She watched Lucy reach for her father's hand. He squeezed it and then reached a hand out to Sophie, to draw her up to her feet.

"What do you say we welcome Sophie to the family with a big old hug?"

Lucy giggled, seeming unsure what to say. Or do.

"Then am I allowed to have my first ride again?"

Sophie and Lark laughed together.

"Yeah, you can ride Cleo again," he told her, before giving her a stern look. "If Doctor Sophie says you can with a cast still on your arm."

Sophie closed her eyes against tears as Lucy wrapped her arms around their waists and hugged them both tightly.

"Of course you can, hon. Of course you can."

Somehow, without knowing why or how she deserved it, Sophie had become part of a family. The kind of family she'd thought she would never have.

Maybe she'd been wrong. Maybe she wasn't being punished for the decisions she'd made, for what she'd done in the past.

Maybe, just maybe, having children of her own hadn't been her destiny.

The family she'd hoped for for so long had been ready-made and waiting for her. And even if it did mean a change of lifestyle, doing something different, she knew in her heart that she would have made the change anyway.

She wasn't doing it because a man had told her to. She wasn't doing it for someone else, to allow someone else to fulfill their dreams and put hers on the back burner.

Marrying Lark would give her the man of *her* dreams, the daughter and lifestyle of *her* dreams, and allow her to figure out what her own career dream was. When she was ready.

"Happy?" Lark asked her.

She smiled up at him. "More than you could ever imagine," she said.

"Oh, you'd be surprised," he said with a laugh.

Then he kissed her, his lips feathering over hers in a motion that threatened to take her breath away.

Again.

EPILOGUE

Sᴏᴘʜɪᴇ arrived home exhausted, but she still managed a smile as she pulled up the driveway. It was funny how the long drive into the property had once filled her stomach with butterflies, made her nervous, when now it made her want to drive faster to walk in the door as quick as she could.

But she didn't even bother going up the steps and putting her key in the door. She knew exactly where to find her family, and it wasn't inside. Not at this time of day and with the sun still shining.

"Lark!" she called.

She needn't have bothered. She saw them before they could have even heard her. Lark was sitting astride his horse, one hand on his knee, the other loosely holding the reins. Lucy was circling around him, fast, hurtling over a series of jumps as he called out instructions and encouragement.

Sophie walked over to them, stopping only to pat a bursting-with-excitement Sam.

"Hey, you," she said, dropping to her knees to give her dog a cuddle. "You been hanging out with your dad all day?"

She grinned at the dog, loving the way his tail wagged so rapidly, tongue lolling out the side of his mouth as he gave her a big canine smile.

"Hey, beautiful."

Sophie rose at Lark's call. He still made her blush, made her skin hot and a tingle form at the base of her spine. Even after a whole year of being with him, looking into her husband's eyes after a long day at work always made her smile.

"You two having fun?"

He nodded his head in Lucy's direction. "Seems she's better than her dad already."

Sophie walked closer to him, hand falling on his leg as she rose on tiptoes to kiss him as he bent.

"Mmm," she murmured.

"How was work?"

"Exhausting, but good at the same time."

It had been a long time since she'd worked in general practice, but the change was good. After fulfilling her contract and working out her last few months until they'd been able to find a replacement surgeon, she'd moved back to open her own practice.

And even though her fingers missed the feel of the scalpel and the environment in the hospital, she was *happy* here with her patients, with her business, with her life.

She looked up at Lark, who had his eyes trained on Lucy again.

But more than being satisfied with her work, she was in love. She'd gone from believing she could never have a family to being welcomed wholeheartedly into one.

She now had a husband *and* a daughter.

And she couldn't have imagined a happier life for herself if she'd tried.

"What do you say we go for a ride?"

"Now?" she asked.

Lark reached down and ran a finger across her cheek.

"Yes, *now,* unless you have something better in mind?"

Sophie laughed at the lazy way he watched her, the faint lines around his eyes and mouth creasing as he tried his hardest not to laugh back at her.

"Oh, there are plenty better things I could imagine doing," she whispered, "but for now a horseback ride will have to do."

Lark winked at her and Sophie slapped him on the thigh.

"Don't tease me, Mrs. Anderson."
"Or what?"
He winked at her. "Just you wait and see."

* * * * *

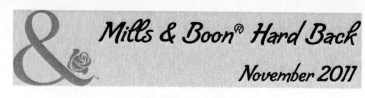

ROMANCE

The Power of Vasilii	Penny Jordan
The Real Rio D'Aquila	Sandra Marton
A Shameful Consequence	Carol Marinelli
A Dangerous Infatuation	Chantelle Shaw
Kholodov's Last Mistress	Kate Hewitt
His Christmas Acquisition	Cathy Williams
The Argentine's Price	Maisey Yates
Captive but Forbidden	Lynn Raye Harris
On the First Night of Christmas...	Heidi Rice
The Power and the Glory	Kimberly Lang
How a Cowboy Stole Her Heart	Donna Alward
Tall, Dark, Texas Ranger	Patricia Thayer
The Secretary's Secret	Michelle Douglas
Rodeo Daddy	Soraya Lane
The Boy is Back in Town	Nina Harrington
Confessions of a Girl-Next-Door	Jackie Braun
Mistletoe, Midwife...Miracle Baby	Anne Fraser
Dynamite Doc or Christmas Dad?	Marion Lennox

HISTORICAL

The Lady Confesses	Carole Mortimer
The Dangerous Lord Darrington	Sarah Mallory
The Unconventional Maiden	June Francis
Her Battle-Scarred Knight	Meriel Fuller

MEDICAL ROMANCE™

The Child Who Rescued Christmas	Jessica Matthews
Firefighter With A Frozen Heart	Dianne Drake
How to Save a Marriage in a Million	Leonie Knight
Swallowbrook's Winter Bride	Abigail Gordon

Mills & Boon® *Large Print*

November 2011

ROMANCE

The Marriage Betrayal	Lynne Graham
The Ice Prince	Sandra Marton
Doukakis's Apprentice	Sarah Morgan
Surrender to the Past	Carole Mortimer
Her Outback Commander	Margaret Way
A Kiss to Seal the Deal	Nikki Logan
Baby on the Ranch	Susan Meier
Girl in a Vintage Dress	Nicola Marsh

HISTORICAL

Lady Drusilla's Road to Ruin	Christine Merrill
Glory and the Rake	Deborah Simmons
To Marry a Matchmaker	Michelle Styles
The Mercenary's Bride	Terri Brisbin

MEDICAL ROMANCE™

Her Little Secret	Carol Marinelli
The Doctor's Damsel in Distress	Janice Lynn
The Taming of Dr Alex Draycott	Joanna Neil
The Man Behind the Badge	Sharon Archer
St Piran's: Tiny Miracle Twins	Maggie Kingsley
Maverick in the ER	Jessica Matthews

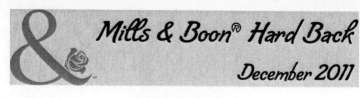

ROMANCE

Jewel in His Crown	Lynne Graham
The Man Every Woman Wants	Miranda Lee
Once a Ferrara Wife...	Sarah Morgan
Not Fit for a King?	Jane Porter
In Bed with a Stranger	India Grey
In a Storm of Scandal	Kim Lawrence
The Call of the Desert	Abby Green
Playing His Dangerous Game	Tina Duncan
How to Win the Dating War	Aimee Carson
Interview with the Daredevil	Nicola Marsh
Snowbound with Her Hero	Rebecca Winters
The Playboy's Gift	Teresa Carpenter
The Tycoon Who Healed Her Heart	Melissa James
Firefighter Under the Mistletoe	Melissa McClone
Flirting with Italian	Liz Fielding
The Inconvenient Laws of Attraction	Trish Wylie
The Night Before Christmas	Alison Roberts
Once a Good Girl...	Wendy S. Marcus

HISTORICAL

The Disappearing Duchess	Anne Herries
Improper Miss Darling	Gail Whitiker
Beauty and the Scarred Hero	Emily May
Butterfly Swords	Jeannie Lin

MEDICAL ROMANCE™

New Doc in Town	Meredith Webber
Orphan Under the Christmas Tree	Meredith Webber
Surgeon in a Wedding Dress	Sue MacKay
The Boy Who Made Them Love Again	Scarlet Wilson

Mills & Boon® Large Print

December 2011

ROMANCE

Bride for Real	Lynne Graham
From Dirt to Diamonds	Julia James
The Thorn in His Side	Kim Lawrence
Fiancée for One Night	Trish Morey
Australia's Maverick Millionaire	Margaret Way
Rescued by the Brooding Tycoon	Lucy Gordon
Swept Off Her Stilettos	Fiona Harper
Mr Right There All Along	Jackie Braun

HISTORICAL

Ravished by the Rake	Louise Allen
The Rake of Hollowhurst Castle	Elizabeth Beacon
Bought for the Harem	Anne Herries
Slave Princess	Juliet Landon

MEDICAL ROMANCE™

Flirting with the Society Doctor	Janice Lynn
When One Night Isn't Enough	Wendy S. Marcus
Melting the Argentine Doctor's Heart	Meredith Webber
Small Town Marriage Miracle	Jennifer Taylor
St Piran's: Prince on the Children's Ward	Sarah Morgan
Harry St Clair: Rogue or Doctor?	Fiona McArthur